COMFORT IN LAVENDER VALLEY

COMFORT IN LAVENDER VALLEY

SISTERS OF THE HEART BOOK 5

TAMMY L. GRACE

LONE MOUNTAIN PRESS

Comfort in Lavender Valley
Sisters of the Heart
Book 5
Tammy L. Grace

www.tammylgrace.com
Facebook: https://www.facebook.com/tammylgrace.books
Twitter: @TammyLGrace
Instagram: @authortammylgrace
Published in the United States by Lone Mountain Press, Nevada

ISBN (eBook) 978-1-945591-61-7
ISBN (Print) 978-1-945591-62-4
FIRST EDITION
Printed in the United States of America
Cover Design by Elizabeth Mackey Graphic Design

ALSO BY TAMMY L. GRACE

COOPER HARRINGTON DETECTIVE NOVELS

Killer Music

Deadly Connection

Dead Wrong

Cold Killer

HOMETOWN HARBOR SERIES

Hometown Harbor: The Beginning (Prequel Novella)

Finding Home

Home Blooms

A Promise of Home

Pieces of Home

Finally Home

Forever Home

Follow Me Home

CHRISTMAS STORIES

A Season for Hope: Christmas in Silver Falls Book 1

The Magic of the Season: Christmas in Silver Falls Book 2

Christmas in Snow Valley: A Hometown Christmas Book 1

One Unforgettable Christmas: A Hometown Christmas Book 2

Christmas Wishes: Souls Sisters at Cedar Mountain Lodge

Christmas Surprises: Soul Sisters at Cedar Mountain Lodge

GLASS BEACH COTTAGE SERIES

Beach Haven

Moonlight Beach

Beach Dreams

WRITING AS CASEY WILSON

A Dog's Hope

A Dog's Chance

WISHING TREE SERIES

The Wishing Tree

Wish Again

Overdue Wishes

SISTERS OF THE HEART SERIES

Greetings from Lavender Valley

Pathway to Lavender Valley

Sanctuary at Lavender Valley

Blossoms at Lavender Valley

Comfort in Lavender Valley

Reunion in Lavender Valley

Remember to subscribe to Tammy's exclusive group of readers for your gift, only available to readers on her mailing list. **Sign up at www.tammylgrace.com. Follow this link to subscribe at https:// wp.me/P9umIy-e** and you'll receive the exclusive interview she did with all the canine characters in her Hometown Harbor Series.

Follow Tammy on Facebook by liking her page. You may also follow Tammy on book retailers or at BookBub by clicking on the follow button.

"The secret to happiness is freedom ... and the secret to freedom is courage."
—*Thucydides*

CHAPTER ONE

As usual, Lydia's timing was less than perfect. She set out for Lavender Valley almost three months ago, but her trusty old motorhome was showing her more than twenty years of age. Gypsy, the name Lydia had christened the Minnie Winnie she'd called home for the last five years, suffered a major transmission malfunction. It happened only about two hours after she left Walla Walla and headed south.

She made it to La Grande, Oregon, a picturesque town in a valley surrounded by the Blue Mountains. Gypsy was acting funny as she maneuvered the steep drop into the town and coasted to a halt only a few feet from an auto repair place, right off the main highway.

The owner, a kind man named Joe, took pity on Lydia and let her stay in the yard behind his shop, until it could be repaired. Lydia's lengthy stay at the garage was directly proportional to her lack of funds and the costly price tag for the transmission work. Within a day, Joe diagnosed the problem and gave Lydia an estimate.

It was jaw dropping, but she didn't have many options since it was her home and only transportation. Lydia was used to finding jobs in the food service arena and within a day, she was employed at a motel within walking distance of the garage.

It was a moderately priced chain that provided a breakfast buffet for guests, and her job was to put out all the food, which was nowhere near her standards, but she set aside her urge to create and did her best with the gross powdered eggs and sticky oatmeal she made each morning. She wasn't hired as the chef. She was basically a cafeteria worker, opening packages of prepared food and pouring juice and coffee. She had to be at work at five in the morning but was done by ten and was off on Sundays and Mondays.

A quick calculation of her pay prompted Lydia to look for a second job. Joe told her about a hole-in-the-wall place looking to hire. The rustic Burger Barn was nothing like the upscale restaurants she usually targeted, but Lydia took an immediate liking to the owner, Nell. The no-nonsense woman was impressed with Lydia's experience and hired her as a cook on the spot. Lydia hoped to work seven days a week to bank her funds, but the Burger Barn was closed on Sundays and Mondays, too.

The restaurant was a few miles away, but Joe was kind enough to loan Lydia an old beater car that he kept in the lockup, and she used it to work the afternoon shift from three o'clock until closing at eight. At least she was actually cooking, albeit a limited menu of burgers, hot dogs, and a couple of sandwich varieties. She did her best to put her own twist on things, artfully displaying the most basic burger with a flair for arranging the veggies and condiments. She made a special tangy sauce that was a huge hit with the customers, both on the burgers and as a dip for french fries.

Lydia often visited with Nell over her free meal and learned she had an interest in starting a food truck for the summer months. Lydia gave Nell lots of advice from her experience doing that for years. She soon discovered Nell and Joe were dating and had been for several years.

Since Joe's wasn't equipped with the typical hookups available in an RV park, water became a bit of an issue. Joe ran an extension cord for her so she could have power, but there was no easy way to hook up to water.

Right next door to the garage was a church, and Joe was on good terms with them. It also didn't hurt that Nell was a longtime member of the congregation. He reached out and asked if Lydia might use their shower facilities, and they agreed. They also had a huge kitchen and to pay back their kindness, she had made a breakfast spread for the fellowship hour after the service on Sundays.

It gave her an outlet for her culinary creations and made her feel better about using their facilities. Each week, they invited her to join them for church, but she always declined. She wasn't good at sitting still and hadn't been inside a church for years. The kitchen at this one was as close as she wanted to get.

Lydia was what Jewel called a free spirit, and she wasn't into organized groups much but couldn't deny how kind the congregation had been to her. They were friendly and never pushy; plus, they were generous with their praise about her food.

She'd reluctantly agreed to meet a few of the ladies, including Nell, to watch a British show, *Vera*, every Monday evening. The fellowship hall was equipped with a large flat-screen television mounted on the wall. Lydia wasn't sure at first, but the main character, an older lady who always wore a trench coat and hat that reminded Lydia of Paddington

Bear, was a gifted detective. A little rough around the edges but lovable.

Lydia looked forward to her Monday night gatherings and made a pot of soup or a hearty salad, plus homemade bread and dessert, which further endeared her in the hearts of the women. The small group, many of them close to Jewel's age, teared up when she said goodbye last Monday. They showered her with gifts and flowers and told her how much they would miss her. Thinking of them, she fingered the silver chain around her neck with the small cross they had given her.

She glanced over in the passenger seat and smiled. The tiny Yorkie, who Lydia named Vera, wandered into the lockup yard one night and adopted Lydia. Although Jewel had imparted her love of animals, and especially dogs, to Lydia, she'd resisted having one. She worked weird hours and didn't want to leave a dog alone so much. She also lived in a motorhome.

The little dog didn't have a collar and wasn't chipped. She looked a little worse for wear and scruffy when Lydia met her, but now she sat with a tiny pink collar encrusted with rhinestones, sporting a pink and brown sweater, resting on her fluffy bed, and looking at Lydia with her sweet eyes. At forty-five, children weren't in Lydia's future. Vera was her only baby. She used to make fun of women with their pampered dogs, but now she understood.

Vera's arrival and her immediate attachment to Lydia made it impossible not to give her a home. Lydia reasoned her size would make it manageable in the motorhome, and her destination at the farm would be perfect for a dog. Not to mention, she fell in love with the tiny bundle of fur the moment she saw her. She relished cuddling with Vera each night and couldn't deny how much happier she was and less lonely since Vera's arrival.

Friday, when she pulled into Lavender Valley, Lydia parked Gypsy, attached Vera's skinny leash, and wandered the downtown area. She spotted the Sugar Shack but didn't go in for fear they might recognize her. She wasn't ready to reconnect and talk about her glory days on television during her stint with the baking contest. So much had happened since then.

She wandered around and checked out the restaurants, which were busy and with the exception of Rooster's, Brick's, the Grasshopper, and the bakery, she didn't remember. The town may have added a few new eateries and shops, but walking along Main Street, Lydia felt like she had stepped back in time thirty years, when she had wandered the same sidewalks.

It was a gorgeous day; the middle of May with Mother's Day having just passed. That made her think of Jewel. She'd been so kind to her and let her make an absolute mess in her kitchen countless times. Tears burned her eyes when she remembered the twinkling sparkle in Jewel's eyes and her delight in eating the special breakfasts she'd made for her each Mother's Day and the beautiful birthday cakes Lydia baked for her. She raved about them for years.

She was so supportive and patient. So unlike her biological mother.

Lydia wandered the shops, noticing all the displays celebrating Mother's Day and the special events from the past weekend advertised on flyers at Wine & Words and the Riverside Grill. Rooster's was even offering free drinks for mothers all week long. The florist's window was filled with gorgeous bouquets, and the pharmacy had a whole window done in shades of lavender and purple. The colors and flowers made Lydia think of Jewel again.

A cute giftshop, Cranberry Cottage, had their display windows decorated with beautiful floral items in soft pinks, peaches, and blues. The soft blue hat, the same color as Lydia's eyes, displayed with the hydrangea tote bag called to her. She might have to come back and check it out.

The downtown area, with its pristine sidewalks, brick buildings, and grassy areas, along with colorful pots and baskets of flowers, reminded Lydia of simpler times. Just being in Lavender Valley felt like a warm hug from Jewel.

She picked up a latte from Winding River Coffee, where the woman behind the counter gave her a bowl of water for Vera. They wandered over to the park and sipped on their refreshments. Lydia worried she might be making a mistake coming back to Lavender Valley but assured herself with each swallow of the milky coffee that she was safe here. Nobody knew about this place or her tie to it.

If she didn't like it, she and Vera could take off and hit the road for their next adventure. That was the beauty of living in a motorhome.

After she finished her coffee, she glanced over at Vera, who was cooling her belly in the soft grass. "Well, Vera, time to go. Are you ready to meet my sisters I never knew I had?"

Vera's head popped up, and she stood, her little bum wiggling. "I'm glad someone's excited," said Lydia.

It didn't take long to drive out of town. She pulled off the road, steeling herself for meeting the women who'd all had the benefit of knowing Jewel and living at the farm. The tattered envelope, stained and curled, held Harry's letter to Lydia and sat on the console next to her. Tears clouded her eyes as she stared at the gate ahead.

Harry's letter was nice and inviting, but it scared Lydia enough to prompt her to leave her job in Walla Walla soon after her boss told her that Harry had called the restaurant. First, she'd taken Gypsy and camped for a couple of weeks before she decided to head somewhere new and drove south in case she chose to wander to Lavender Valley. She'd had plenty of time while stuck in La Grande to research Harry and found the many articles in the Salem newspapers with her photo and comments related to her work with the police.

She should have contacted Harry long before now, but Lydia had mastered the skill of being unpredictable. She never let anyone get too close and since she never had a firm plan, it was easy to keep her future schedule a secret. Where she ended up was always a surprise. Even to her.

It wasn't the way most people operated, but it worked for Lydia. She had learned the hard way, but after her last horrible relationship, one in a long string of many, she vowed to sink even deeper underground.

Jewel had been the person in Lydia's life who had never wavered. Guilt tugged at her heart as she thought about all the lovely letters she had received from her and all the times Lydia intended to write back or promised to visit, yet never made it back to the farm in recent years.

She'd let Jewel down, and tears streaked down her cheeks as she waited for her confidence to build so she could press the button on the intercom. Vera whined a bit and reached her paw out to comfort Lydia.

The stake in the farm was such a kind gesture from Jewel, but Lydia had no intention of staying in one place for too long. Missing the April deadline Harry mentioned wasn't important to her. She only hoped her sisters of the heart would understand and forgive her for her tardiness.

She sighed and turned the key in the ignition. Gypsy rumbled to life, and Lydia pulled up to the pedestal with the intercom. She hesitated and glanced back at Vera before she pushed the button. "Let's hope this is the right decision, Vera."

CHAPTER TWO

Lydia's buzz was answered by a woman's voice asking if she could help her. Lydia leaned closer to the speaker. "Uh, I'm looking for Harry, Harriet. I'm Lydia Morrow."

"Lydia! We've been wondering where you were. Come on up the driveway." The gate opened.

She glanced over at Vera, who was standing up on her bed, looking out the window. Her tiny bum wiggled with excitement as she took in the scenery.

As Lydia steered her motorhome in front of the farmhouse, she spotted a tall woman waving. "Harry," she whispered, recognizing her from the photos she found in the newspaper.

Harry motioned her to the side and then hurried to the driver's window. Lydia smiled at her. "Where's the best place to park? I don't want to be in the way of anyone."

Harry glanced over her shoulder. "You probably need power?" She raised her eyebrows. "I think next to that first cottage would be best." She pointed at the blank space next to it.

Lydia nodded. "Yes, I need power. That looks like a great spot."

Harry pointed at the passenger seat. "Looks like you've got a copilot who will fit right in around here. Olivia is our resident dog expert. She's in the shelter right now. I'll run and tell her you're here."

Lydia maneuvered Gypsy along the side of the cottage, making sure the side with her power cord was closest to the building and turned off the ignition. She sighed and scooped up Vera. "Let's go introduce ourselves."

Worried she might forget to plug Gypsy in, Lydia took the time to retrieve the power cord and adapter and plugged it into the outlet on the side of the cottage. She let Vera sniff along the grass and do her business before leading her toward the house.

As they walked near the porch, she noticed Harry waiting, and then another woman, even taller, came from around the back of the house. Her dark hair was in a ponytail, and she smiled and bent down to greet Vera. At five feet seven inches, Lydia always considered herself on the tall side, but these two women towered over her.

"Hey there, aren't you a sweet girl." Olivia reached out her hand, and Vera hurried over to her. Olivia laughed and glanced up at Lydia. "I'm Olivia, by the way. I'm so glad you're here. What a wonderful surprise."

"It's great to meet you, Olivia." She caught Harry's eye and added, "I'm sorry for not calling ahead… or at all."

Harry tilted her head toward the house. "Come on in and relax. Micki isn't home right now but will be back later tonight. We don't have much planned for dinner, so we might have to dash to town and pick something up."

Lydia followed Vera, who was tugging at her leash to get closer to Olivia. They filed into the house, and Olivia pointed across to the sunroom on the other side of the living area. "I've got the dogs out in the yard. I didn't want to overwhelm Vera on her first day with us."

Lydia grinned at the little dog. "She acts like a big dog until things get serious." Her eyes went to the kitchen, and she stepped through the dining room and stood in the middle of it.

She surveyed the entire room and said, "Wow. This is gorgeous and so much bigger than before. Look at those double ovens." Her blue eyes twinkled as she opened the doors on each of them to get a closer look.

Harry gave her a sheepish grin. "Totally wasted on me. Olivia is better at cooking, but I'm a lost cause."

With a wave of her hand, Olivia motioned them to the living area. "Let's sit down, and then we can let Vera get to know our dogs. I've got a couple in the shelter that are more her size."

Harry rested her hands on the back of the sofa. "Our goldens are sweethearts. I brought Chief with me from Salem, Hope was Jewel's last dog, and Olivia adopted Willow. You can introduce Vera when you're ready. We've got iced tea if you'd like one?"

"Yes, that sounds great. We've been on the road since before six this morning and only stopped a few times."

Olivia frowned, "That's a long day." She retrieved a bowl of water for Vera, and her little tongue lapped it up. "I'll run into town and get some dinner for us. What sounds good to you, Lydia? With you being a chef, I'm sure you're used to fancy meals. We've got some good places, but they're probably not up to your standards."

Lydia laughed. "I love cooking and eating, and I'm really not that picky. In fact, I'd love to cook for all of you when Micki's home. Maybe Sunday night? Consider it an apology dinner for being inconsiderate and not letting you know when I was coming."

Harry delivered glasses of iced tea and laughed. "Well, I'm a rotten cook, so I'll take you up on your offer to cook anytime, but no apology needed. We were just worried about you. When you left Walla Walla, I couldn't find you."

Vera's tiny nails on the wood floor announced her arrival from the kitchen. She hurried to Lydia and rested at her feet.

After a long swallow from her glass, Lydia sighed. "I should have called. I'm terrible about things like that, and I had every intention of being here long before now. Gypsy broke down in Le Grande. I've been there for about two months."

Olivia's forehead creased. "Gypsy?"

Lydia laughed. "That's my motorhome. And, I'm a bit of a wanderer. I have a hard time staying in one place for long."

Harry set her glass on a coaster. "We've got another wrinkle in our original plan. Micki and Olivia are staying upstairs. Micki's daughter Meg is visiting her for the summer and is staying in the other bedroom, which is technically yours."

Lydia raised her hand. "Don't give it a thought. I live in my motorhome, and that's where I'll stay. I plugged her in and stopped at a dump station on my way, so my tanks are empty. I just need to fill it with water or hook up to water, and I'll be set."

Olivia and Harry both shook their heads. Olivia was the first to speak. "Oh, Micki will be beside herself to think you're having to live in your motorhome."

Vera stood on her back legs and put a tiny paw on Lydia's calf. She picked her up and put the dog on her lap. "Honestly, I prefer it. Not to say I won't take advantage of that kitchen or a long, hot shower occasionally, but I'm really happy in it. It's home."

Harry met Lydia's eyes. "It's a shame you didn't call us before the end of April. We could have worked something out with Jewel's attorney. I hate to have you miss out on your share of the farm."

Lydia stroked Vera's back. "Honestly, I have no intention of staying here long-term. I should have called, but not for the legal reasons. Jewel told me I have itchy feet, and I think she was right." Her throat tightened around her words.

She took a drink from her glass. "It's weird being here. I keep thinking Jewel will walk in any minute." Tears filled her eyes. "I didn't keep in touch like I should have and could have come back and visited, but I never made the time."

Olivia nodded at her. "We all have many of those same regrets. The best intentions, but not the best follow through, for me. Life gets in the way sometimes, and I didn't make it a priority. I don't think I realized how much I enjoyed her letters and phone calls."

Harry gestured toward the bookcase. "Her old journals are here if you're interested in reading them. A tad bittersweet, but interesting to read her thoughts and impressions of all the foster children she took in over her life."

Lydia took a deep breath. "I think I'll have to work up to that."

"You mentioned not wanting to stay too long, but we hope you'll stay for the festival." Olivia arched her brows. "Not to guilt you into it, but I think we could use the help. Micki is the driving force and has some great ideas and additions."

Harry nodded and added, "Oh, and we haven't even told you about Georgia. She'll be here next month, we hope. She was on her way when she fell at the home she just sold and hurt her shoulder. She's staying with a friend until she can drive from Boise."

Lydia hung her head. "Now, I really wish I would have called. I could have picked her up on my way."

Harry shook her head. "I doubt that would have worked. She's bringing her car and wouldn't have wanted to leave it there. We had a video chat with her, which was great. Maybe we can do that again and include you?"

"Sure." Lydia bobbed her head as she continued to pet Vera. "I'll stay for the festival for sure. I'm just not sure about staying the rest of the year."

Olivia clapped her hands together. "Well, that's great news. Now, we better figure out dinner before it gets any later. We don't need to worry about Micki and Meg tonight, so it's just the three of us."

Lydia leaned back against the cushions. "I'm game for anything. I've spent the last two months putting out the free breakfast offerings at a small hotel and manning the grill at the Burger Barn, so my cooking is not always fancy. I love a good burger or grilled cheese."

Harry stood and said, "I'll run into town and grab something from Rooster's. It will be the quickest option."

"Sounds perfect," said Lydia.

"While Harry's doing that, how about we go outside and introduce Vera to a few friends?" Olivia collected their empty glasses and dropped them off in the kitchen. Harry collected her purse and promised to be back soon.

Lydia attached Vera's leash, and they followed Olivia to the sunroom.

Olivia pointed out the window. "Our three goldens are

gentle. Hope is wonderful with all the new rescues, and Willow is learning from her. Chief belonged to Harry's old partner who passed away, and he's also picking up on things from Hope and helps acclimate my new dogs." She led the way outside to the back porch.

The three dogs came running over to the gate, tails wagging. Olivia glanced down at Vera and saw her bum wiggling. "She seems at ease with them, what do you think?"

Lydia shrugged. "I don't know much about dogs, and she's only been around one other dog since I found her but did fine. Like I said, she sometimes barks and acts tough when she's far away or sees a dog from her perch in the window."

Olivia took the leash Lydia offered and guided Vera through the gate. The three goldens got down on their bellies, their tails still wagging with excitement. Vera bounced between the trio, sniffing at each of them.

After the inspection, the four of them wandered to the middle of the grass, with Hope being the first to get down on her belly, her backside up high, where she tried to get Vera to play. It didn't take long before Vera was darting toward her, placing her tiny paws on top of Hope's.

"Aww," said Lydia, reaching down to pet all the goldens. "What loves they are. I'm so glad Vera will have some friends. She's been stuck with me this whole time. Joe, the owner of the garage and the guy who fixed my motorhome, let me stay there in his lockup yard, and he watched over Vera when I was at work. He had a dog who played with her."

"I think dogs need to have dog friends. She'll have lots to do here on the farm, and I can't wait until she meets Thelma and Milton. They're on the smaller size and still getting settled in here. I actually had two Yorkies here but found a home for them recently."

Lydia gazed across the yard and pointed at the garden. "Someone's been busy. That garden looks great."

"That's Micki's handiwork. She's the only one with a green thumb. She also planted a nice kitchen herb garden that will be of interest to you. It's right outside the mudroom."

"There's nothing like fresh herbs. They really make all the difference in dishes." She watched over Vera as she played and romped with the big dogs. As Lydia leaned on the fence, she sighed. "It really is peaceful here."

Olivia stood from her crouched position watching the dogs. "I had my doubts coming here, but it's almost like slipping into a comfy pair of old slippers. It just feels right. I was at the lowest point in my life when I decided to come and as we always say, Jewel seems to be watching over us even now. I've found a new purpose here and even more, I've found hope."

"Hmm... hope. That's something I haven't felt for a long time. It seems like I'm always playing catch up and struggling to figure things out. I avoid thinking about tomorrow."

Olivia rested her hand on Lydia's arm. "Give yourself some time. You can relax here and rest. We've all had our struggles. Micki is in the midst of one of her own right now. She and Meg are at the hospital in Medford visiting Micki's sister. They've been estranged for decades. It's a long story, and I'll let her share it when she's ready. We're all doing our best to support her."

"Oh, that sounds complicated." Lydia glanced over at Olivia. "It's nice that you're all there for her. Outside of Jewel and Chuck, I've never been able to rely on anyone. I've gotten used to being on my own." She paused and looked off into the distance. "Being in La Grande for so long, I did make a few friends. My boss at the burger place helped me get permission to use the church next door for showering. To pay them back, I volunteered to make their fellowship breakfasts each week and got close to several of the ladies. They were really kind to me."

"That's lovely. I've been going to church with my friend Duke and his family. His sister May owns a store downtown, Cranberry Cottage. He's the local veterinarian and a wonderful guy." She blushed and smiled. "We're dating, which at our age, is a strange thing to say."

Lydia grinned at Olivia and pressed her shoulder into hers. "That's awesome, and I noticed that store when I stopped in town today. It's really cute, and their display made me want to come back and check out some of their stuff. At the moment, I'm not exactly flush with cash. I need to find a job before I treat myself to anything."

"I'm sure one of the local eateries would be happy to have you on staff. I don't think they have many experienced chefs in the area."

"I'll run into town tomorrow. I need to go by the market and get some things for Sunday's dinner." She stretched her back and stood taller. "Oh and be sure to invite Duke."

"While we're talking about inviting others, we should also include Clay and Heath, the brothers who run the ranch next door. They were devoted to Jewel and excited to meet you. Clay and Harry are an item." She grinned and held up her finger. "And Buck Simpson, Jewel's attorney. He and Micki have become quite close. He's taking her on a getaway this weekend, but they'll be home Sunday."

"The more the merrier, I always say. I always make plenty but will keep that in mind."

"And before you go shopping, check the freezer. The Nolan Ranch provides us with all the beef we want, and it's full right now. Oh, and tomorrow is the farmer's market. You might want to check it out."

"Wow, I'll do that. I'd love to get some local produce. I'll take a look in the freezer first and see what inspires me."

Olivia checked her watch. "Harry should be back soon. Let's get this crew inside and feed them their dinner, and you can check out the freezer and pantry."

Lydia dashed to her motorhome to collect Vera's food and treats and met Olivia in the mudroom where all their furry friends waited patiently for their bowls to be filled.

Olivia checked out Vera's bag of food. "Are you open to transitioning her to a different food? There's a higher quality one I've been feeding the dogs, and it would take a few weeks to get her used to it but would make feeding times easier."

Lydia nodded. "Sure, I didn't research this brand, just chose it because of the price point."

"I'll take care of feeding her with the others and slowly work her into this other food. I doctor up their bowls with bits of extra meat and blueberries. Does she have any issues with any foods?"

Lydia shook her head. "No, not that I've noticed." She watched as Olivia talked to each of the dogs and told them how much she loved them as she fixed their meal.

As she filled a small bowl for Vera, making sure she had just a small portion of the new food mixed with her old, Olivia said, "We'll need to give you a tour of the farm and the house." She pointed across the room. "Washer and dryer are in here, and we all do our own laundry."

"I need to do some laundry, so that's great."

Olivia made all the dogs wait while she placed their bowls down on a mat. Then she gave them the command, and they commenced gobbling. Vera looked lost for a few minutes but picked up on the cues from the others.

Lydia followed Olivia into the living area. "Television is there, and Harry's got it hooked up to her account for streaming services." She pointed toward the front door. "We've got an intercom system on the front gate. I'll give you the code you can use to enter. We changed it recently, so it's limited to just us along with Duke, Clay, Heath, and Buck. Oh, and Tyler, he's the ranch hand that lives here in the bunkhouse."

Olivia continued wandering through the house, pointing out the sunroom and Micki's desk, Harry's bedroom and bathroom, the downstairs powder room and then upstairs where the three guest bedrooms shared a large bathroom.

Lydia sucked in a breath when she looked into Olivia's bedroom. "It's just like I remember." She walked to the window and touched the eyelet curtains. The scent of lavender tickled her nose. "Gosh, it even smells like Jewel in here."

Olivia pointed at the jar of cream on her nightstand. "Micki has us sampling some of the lavender products she wants to carry for the festival and the website. We'll get you some to try, too."

Tears dripped onto Lydia's cheeks. "I can't believe Jewel's gone."

Olivia slipped an arm around Lydia's shoulder. "I know. Even though I hadn't seen her in a long time, I feel like a piece of me is gone with her."

Lydia gulped down a sob. "She was my only family."

Olivia smiled and gripped her tighter. "Not anymore. You've got us. Your sisters of the heart."

CHAPTER THREE

The scent of fresh grass with a hint of floral notes wafted through the open window of Lydia's bedroom. She opened her eyes to sunlight streaming through the water-spotted glass and reached over to pet the top of Vera's silky head.

Exhausted from the drive and the emotional toll of being back under Jewel's roof, but without Jewel, she and Vera elected to turn in early last night. Micki and Meg hadn't yet returned home, but Lydia was too tired to wait for them. She managed to get a load of laundry done while they ate dinner and visited but needed to do her sheets and towels today. She also needed to give Gypsy a bath and a good cleaning.

After a long stretch, Lydia climbed off the bed and took two steps to reach the tiny bathroom. Last night, Harry insisted Lydia share the master bathroom with her and make use of the amenities, including the full-sized shower. As much as Lydia protested the idea, as she looked at the cramped quarters, she packed up her toiletries, grabbed some clean clothes, and tucked Vera under her arm. She descended the steps and headed toward the house, taking in the golden glow of the morning sun on the pastures.

A long, hot shower, with an unlimited water supply, sounded heavenly. She made her way to the mudroom door and found Olivia working on breakfast for the dogs. "Morning," said Lydia.

"How'd you sleep?" Olivia sprinkled blueberries on top of each bowl.

"Really well. I was so tired last night and feel much better today. I'm just going to slip in and take a shower."

Olivia gestured to the kitchen. "Harry's already up and at it, having coffee." She reached and took Vera from Lydia. "I'll get this little gal fed her breakfast. You take as long as you need."

Lydia stepped into the kitchen where Harry was sipping coffee and scrolling on her tablet. "Morning, Harry." She held up her toiletry bag. "I decided to take you up on your offer and grab a shower."

"That's wonderful. It's all set for you. Fresh towels are on the rack. Breakfast should be ready when you're done."

Lydia hurried across the living area and to the master bedroom. The lovely aroma of lavender hung in the air, and she noticed the same jar of lavender-infused body butter she saw in Olivia's room on the bathroom counter.

She took her time and let the warm water soak into her neck and shoulders. She helped herself to a scoop of the lavender salt scrub she found in the shower and closed her eyes to inhale the fresh scent. She emerged feeling much better. She went about brushing her teeth and drying off before slipping into jeans and a blue shirt that matched her eyes.

She left her long hair to air dry, slipping the scrunchie she used to secure it onto her wrist. Lydia was always running late and never had time for makeup. She swiped a bit of lip gloss over her lips and deemed herself ready for the day.

When she entered the kitchen, she found Harry and Olivia working on breakfast and two women seated at the granite counter. They both smiled at her, and Lydia noticed how much the two of them looked alike. She took a few steps toward them and extended her hand. "You must be Micki. I'm Lydia. I'm so sorry I couldn't wait up to meet you last night."

Micki smiled and bypassed the hand and went for a hug instead. She squeezed Lydia tightly. "We're so glad you're here. I'm sorry we were so late last night. We stayed at the hospital until visiting hours ended and then stopped to grab something to eat in Medford."

"I'm sorry to hear about your sister. I hope she's feeling better soon."

"Thank you." Micki lowered her voice to a whisper, "I'll tell you the whole story later." She released Lydia, reached across her chair, and gestured to the young woman next to it. "This is my daughter Meg."

Lydia stretched her hand out across the empty chair. "Hi, Meg. It's great to meet you. Olivia says you're working at the veterinary clinic for the summer."

Her smile widened. "Yeah, I've got to head out in a few minutes."

Olivia added a platter of bacon to the counter, and Harry followed with a bowl of scrambled eggs. Micki pointed at Meg's plate. "Go ahead and eat, Meg, so you can get to work."

Olivia slid a bowl of fruit closer to her. "This one," she pointed at Meg, "had Vera on her lap most of the time you were taking a shower."

"She's a charmer. That's how I ended up with her." Lydia helped herself to a plate.

Meg spooned the rest of her eggs onto a slice of toast and folded it, hurrying out the door. "I'll see you tomorrow, Mom. Have a good time."

Micki followed her outside and returned to the kitchen a few minutes later. She went about filling her plate and joined the other three at the dining table. "I feel bad that I'm going to miss out on your first full day with us. I'll give you a tour of the fields and the garden when I get home." She hurried to her purse and retrieved a set of keys. "Before I forget, Harry and Olivia mentioned you have a motorhome, but I wanted to offer the use of my car this weekend. If you need to run to town or anything."

Lydia took the keys, and her heart swelled. "That's so kind of you, but I'm used to driving Gypsy."

Micki shook her head. "I won't be using it, so if you need it, just take it. It's much easier to maneuver downtown."

Lydia slipped the keys into her pocket. "Thank you. I do need to run to the market. I'm cooking for everyone tomorrow night. Be sure to invite Buck to join us."

Harry reached for a slice of toast. "I let Clay and Heath know you were treating us to a special dinner, and they'll be here."

Olivia smiled. "Duke, too. Are you sure that's not too many people? We don't want to overwhelm you."

Lydia finished a bite of the eggs. "These are really good. And, no, a Sunday dinner won't overwhelm me. I've already decided on a menu and took some meat out of the freezer."

Harry placed her silverware across her empty plate. "I'd offer to help, but the best I can do is clean up the dishes."

Olivia nodded. "Yes, if there's anything we can do to help, just say the word."

Lydia reached for her cup. "I think I've got it covered, but

I'll definitely take you up on the cleanup duties. That's my least favorite part of cooking."

Micki checked her watch. "Buck will be here in a few minutes, but you can count on me for dish duty, too."

"Where are you headed for your weekend getaway?" asked Lydia.

"Not far. Buck has tickets for a wine tasting and music event at the Dragonfly Estate. He was able to get the last two rooms at the inn, which looks fabulous from their website. They're doing a dinner tonight with the wine tasting. We should be home by mid-afternoon tomorrow."

"That sounds lovely. I hope you have a great time," said Lydia, scooping up her last bite from her plate. "I'll take care of the breakfast dishes since Olivia and Harry made breakfast."

Olivia grinned. "I won't say no to that offer. I have to admit, it's intimidating to cook for a chef."

Lydia brushed away her concern with a wave of her hand. "Don't be silly. It was delicious and for the most part, I make and eat simple stuff. This was perfect."

Micki excused herself and went to gather her things. Olivia pointed outside. "When you're ready, I'd love to show you around the shelter and the farm. I'll leave the flowers and fields to Micki."

"That sounds great. All I have planned is a trip to the market." She gathered the breakfast dishes.

Harry wandered over to the rug where all the goldens were stretched out, and Vera was snuggled next to Hope. "It looks like Vera is settling right in with her new friends." She bent down to pet them all, giving Vera special attention. "I also feel bad about leaving you today, but I had plans to take a drive with Clay. He's looking at a horse."

Adding soap to the sponge, Lydia shook her head. "Don't

worry about it. I should have called, and I don't expect all of you to cancel your plans because of me. I'll be fine and look forward to some quiet time and exploring downtown."

Harry swallowed the last of her coffee and took her cup to the sink. "I won't be home until late tonight, so if I miss you, I'll see you in the morning. You're in excellent hands with Olivia. She'll probably have you playing with the goats and her pet lamb in no time."

Olivia laughed as she gathered the rest of the dishes and brought them to the sink. "Yes, introducing Lydia to all the animals is on our agenda today. I'm also going to give everyone a bath if I can manage it."

As Lydia slid a pan under the faucet, water sprayed up and drenched her face and shirt. She laughed and looked over at Olivia. "I can help you with that. It looks like I'm dressed for it. I just need to run up to the farmer's market first."

"Oh, yes. It's downtown at the park. You can't miss it." She pointed outside. "Buck's here, and I'm dog-sitting Stubbs, so I'll run to collect him and introduce him to your Vera."

Harry and Micki shouted out their goodbyes as they headed out the door. The dogs hurried to watch, lined up in front of the glass portion of the door, except for Vera, who couldn't reach it.

A few minutes later, Olivia came through the door with Stubbs, sporting one of his bowties. Lydia couldn't help but stop what she was doing to meet him. She collected Vera and held her close while Olivia spoke to Stubbs in a quiet voice.

He looked up at Lydia with his big, brown eyes while his cute bum wiggled with excitement. Vera craned her neck forward, anxious to sniff the newcomer. Olivia petted the top of Stubbs' head. "He's a friendly one. Go ahead and put Vera down, and we'll see how they do together."

After a few sniffs, they were besties and wandered off to join the goldens, who were sprawled on their rug. "He's such a cutie," said Lydia, reaching to rinse the last of the dishes.

"He belonged to a woman who passed away, and I thought he was the perfect dog for Buck. Turns out it was a great match."

Olivia had the counters wiped down by the time Lydia finished drying the last of the pans. She hung the wet towel on the bar across the front of the dishwasher. "Do you mind if I leave Vera here with you while I run into town?"

Olivia shook her head. "Not at all. I'll take her and Stubbs out and let them get to know Thelma and Milton. We'll be fine. Take your time." She touched the pocket of her jeans. "We should exchange cell phone numbers, just in case you need anything."

Lydia nodded. "I left mine in the motorhome but give me yours, and I'll text you when I get to mine."

Olivia wrote her number on a sticky note and handed it to her. She glanced at the wet blotches on Lydia's shirt. "You'll probably dry off by the time you get to town."

Lydia grabbed the hem and waved it, trying to create a breeze to dry it. "I think I'll pop in a load of laundry before I leave, if that's okay?"

"Sure, and you don't need to ask. Just make yourself at home."

By the time Lydia parked Micki's car, the dark splotches on her shirt had faded, and she looked none the worse for wear. She added a baseball cap over her hair and threaded her ponytail through the hole in the back of it.

She slung her purse strap across her body and walked to

the park. It was filled with colorful canopies above vendors selling fresh produce along with crafts and homemade items. Lydia took a basket from a stack near the entrance and perused the offerings.

She selected a variety of mushrooms, fresh arugula, tomatoes, onions, garlic, lemons, and a flat of the most delicious strawberries she'd tasted in a long time. She walked past a local cheesemaker and tasted several of their samples. She was wowed by the rosemary cheddar and bought a block along with some goat cheese. As she left, munching on another sample atop a cracker, she wandered the stalls in search of one more ingredient. As she was gawking, she ran into the back of a tall man.

He turned around and tipped his cowboy hat up a bit, revealing a set of blue eyes Lydia couldn't help staring at. She finally remembered her manners. "I'm so sorry. I wasn't watching where I was going."

He grinned. "Not a problem." He lifted his hat off his head for a moment. "Have a nice day."

Embarrassed and feeling the heat rise in her cheeks, she turned at the next aisle and stopped at another fruit stand, tempted by the offer of a sample of their blackberries. After a bite, she couldn't resist and bought two baskets. As the woman gave her change, Lydia asked if there was a truffle oil vendor anywhere at the market. The woman shook her head. "Your best bet is Cranberry Cottage. They carry several specialty oils."

She made her way across the park and stashed her bags in the footwell of the passenger seat before hurrying down and across the street to Cranberry Cottage. It was bustling with shoppers, no doubt spilling over from the market.

A petite woman wearing a black wrist brace turned from straightening a display and caught Lydia's eye. "Welcome in.

I'm May, one of the owners. Is there anything I can help you find?"

"I'm Lydia, and I'm staying out at Jewel's farm. Olivia mentioned you." She smiled and added, "I'm searching for truffle oil."

The woman's eyes brightened. "It's wonderful to meet you, Lydia. I'm sure the others are glad you arrived. Follow me for truffle oil." She led Lydia over to a corner of the store where soup mixes, bread mixes, and kitchen gadgets were displayed.

Lydia pointed at May's leg. "It looks like you've been through the wringer."

She smiled. "I had a fight with a ladder and lost." She pointed at the cabinet where a variety of flavored oils and vinegars were lined up on display. "You can sample any of these you like."

"I love to cook with flavored oils, so I could spend all day here tasting." She fingered the bottle of truffle oil. "I better just take this and get back home. I've got a car full of produce." She looked around and spied the pretty hydrangea bag and the blue hat. "Not to mention, I could outspend my wallet on so many things. You've got a great selection."

"Thank you and come back anytime," said May, hobbling back toward the register. They chatted while May tapped the buttons on the electronic pad.

"I'm making dinner for everyone tomorrow and need this oil for a mushroom risotto." Lydia eyed the price on the register. "That's not right. It's less than it should be."

May grinned. "Consider it a welcome home discount. We're so glad you're here, Lydia."

The words caught in Lydia's throat as she pulled bills out of her wallet. "That's really very kind of you. I appreciate it." She took the change and added, "If you hear of any of the local restaurants looking for a chef, let me know. I need to get some work while I'm here."

"It's the start of our busy season with lots of tourist traffic. I'd suggest visiting the Ranch House. They're our most upscale place, and the Riverside Grille is always a good bet. Clay and Heath Nolan could introduce you to the owners of the Ranch House. It's owned by a husband-and-wife team, and they buy all their beef from the ranch. They restored a beautiful old Victorian. It's right at the end of Main as it turns to residential."

"Oh, great. That's good to know. I'll follow up on that. Thanks, May." Lydia took the bottle and waved away the offer of a bag. "It was great to meet you."

"Come back and visit again." May pointed at another woman with long, dark hair, helping a customer with some of their handmade soap. "That's Janet, my business partner. When we're not busy, we're always up for a chat and a glass of wine or iced tea."

"I'll make a point of it. Thanks again," said Lydia, making her way out the door. She stopped at the deli for prosciutto and then steered Micki's SUV down Main in the direction May had explained. She saw the stately Victorian home with the sign out front. She slowed and pulled to the curb, taking in the groomed grounds and the colorful flowers potted on the porch.

She could see herself working there. Hopefully, an introduction from her neighbors would get her an interview, and then she could wow them with some of her best dishes. She pulled away and glanced at her phone sticking out of her purse. It was time to buy a new one.

She turned and headed back to the convenience store connected to the gas station she remembered. She parked, hurried inside, and emerged with a new flip phone loaded with enough minutes to get her by until it was time to change phones again.

She headed back to the farm, anxious to borrow a laptop or tablet from one of the ladies and have a look at the restaurants online and study their menus. She made a point of staying offline, and her phone was only for calls and texts. Sometimes, it was overwhelming, but so far, her plan had worked to keep her safe, and she didn't want to jeopardize it now.

CHAPTER FOUR

Once home, Lydia washed and stored the veggies and put the berries in the fridge. Then, she took her new phone to the motorhome where she plugged it in and wrote down the number for Olivia.

Lydia found her in the shelter building, where she was busy giving Willow a bath. "Sorry, my phone was dead, so here's my number. It's charging now."

Olivia looked up from scrubbing and smiled. "You're just in time. Willow is my first victim today. You can leave that note in the office by my desk." She gestured to Stubbs, who was lying on the floor watching. "He's clean and doesn't need a bath. He spends most of his day in Buck's office."

Lydia took the note to the office. She hated lying to Olivia about her phone, but if she mentioned the burner phone, questions would ensue. Once back in the room, they worked together to hold and rinse Willow, who was calm and cooperative throughout the entire process. They dried her with a towel and transferred her out of the tub and to the counter where Olivia went about using the blower to dry her.

While she did that, Lydia went out into the yard and scooped up Vera for a bath. She went about working the soap into her while Olivia finished drying Willow. Once Willow was mostly dry, Olivia attached a lavender bandana around her neck and put her collar back on her.

"Oh, she looks so pretty," said Lydia, looking over her shoulder as she rinsed Vera, who was giving her a side eye, letting her know how unimpressed she was with the operation.

Olivia showed her how to use the blower to dry the petite dog. Vera was not a fan of it, but as Lydia talked to her and reassured her, she was able to use the lowest setting and get her dry. Olivia already had a small bandana set out for Vera, another lavender one. Olivia led them and Stubbs to the playroom and set out some balls and toys to keep them busy until their friends joined them.

Next up was Hope, who was used to being bathed and cooperated fully by turning when asked and closed her eyes as they rinsed her, as if she enjoyed it. Like Willow, she seemed to like the free massage that came with towel drying the best but tolerated the blow dryer.

Bathing Chief was more of a struggle session. Olivia laughed as he managed to shake water all over her. "He's not quite as used to having a bath as the other two, but he gets less anxious each time."

With the big dogs done, dried, and outfitted with their lavender bandanas, it was time to tackle Thelma and Milton. Both of them shook and were beyond scared, but Olivia stroked them and talked to them as Lydia helped hold each of them. After more than two solid hours of work, they had six clean dogs and Stubbs in the playroom. Thelma, in her yellow polka-dotted bandana, perked right up and joined the others chasing the ball. Milton, wearing a green bandana, was a little standoffish.

Together, Lydia and Olivia made quick work of cleaning up the tub and counters and joined the dogs with a game of fetch. Milton warmed up and like Stubbs, enjoyed the squeaker toys, pouncing on them whenever Lydia made them squeal. Vera was enjoying herself darting among all the dogs and found a soft toy she claimed as her own.

Once the dogs were tuckered out, Olivia posed Thelma and Milton for their adoption photos; both of them looked charming with their brightly colored bandanas. She wanted to give them more time to settle before she solicited pet parents, but they were so cute and clean, she couldn't resist the photo op.

Lydia helped her guide the dogs back to their comfy stables. Olivia looked over at Lydia and then down at her own clothes. "What a mess we are. I was going to take you out to see the other animals." She looked down at the flipflops Lydia was wearing. "I meant to tell you, you'll probably want to wear a pair of boots when you're out and about on the farm. My feet are huge, so I had to buy a pair, but you might be able to find some that fit in the mudroom. Jewel had an assortment."

Lydia chuckled as she gazed down at her drenched shirt and jeans. "Yeah, boots are probably a better idea. I'd like to get out of these damp clothes anyway. I'll run and change and meet you inside and take a look at those boots."

"I'll get these five settled in the house," offered Olivia, picking up Vera and leading the other dogs out the door.

Lydia added her wet clothes to the pile of laundry she still needed to do and slipped into a clean T-shirt and exercise pants. Her new phone was charged, and she slipped it into the side pocket of her pants and gathered the load of laundry.

She transferred her clean load to the dryer and added in the clothes to wash before stepping into the kitchen, where she found Olivia sipping iced tea. She pointed at the full glass next to hers. "I poured you one, too."

She slid into the chair next to Olivia and took a long swallow. "You've done an incredible job with the shelter. That's a real workout with those dogs."

"I appreciate the help. I normally don't bathe all of them in one swoop, but it's great to have it done." She pointed over at the five of them, sprawled across the area rug, sleeping. "I think we wore them out."

Lydia smiled at them, noting Vera tucked up close between Stubbs and Hope. "I think Vera likes her new friends." She lowered her voice and said, "I remember Jewel letting me make them homemade dog treats. I could try it again and if they're a hit, we could sell them at the festival. Along that same line, I was thinking of some fun recipes that I could use and incorporate lavender. Like cookies, muffins, cupcakes, and lavender pairs well with lemon. Oh, and I've done a lavender and blackberry cheesecake. I could make some minis for us to sample."

"Oh, that sounds divine. Micki will be thrilled to hear your ideas."

Lydia took another sip and sighed. "I'm actually excited to create them. I haven't been able to spend much time doing that lately. The last couple of months have been hard, but when I was at the market today, I was thinking about using lavender as a theme and coming up with some fun things we could sell at the festival. I've got that little buzz of excitement going that comes with a new project."

"That's wonderful," said Olivia, nodding toward the

fridge. "If you're getting hungry, we've got some leftovers in there."

Lydia shook her head. "I'm fine. That breakfast filled me up. I don't normally eat much in the morning."

"With it being just the two of us tonight, are you okay with leftovers? Meg is going out with a couple of coworkers from Duke's clinic, so she won't be here."

Lydia nodded. "Leftovers sound perfect. We'll figure something out. If you're up to it, we can check out the other animals, and then I need to finish my laundry."

"Sounds great. We'll let sleeping dogs lie, as they say." Olivia pointed to the dogs and led the way to the mudroom. As she slipped into her boots, and Lydia found a pair that fit, she whispered, "They'll wake as soon as they hear us leave, but I want to keep them clean at least for the rest of the day."

She led the way around to the front of the house and across to the pen in front of the barn, where the donkeys were grazing. Lydia pointed at the sunflower mural. "That is beautiful."

"Oh, Micki did that. She planted sunflowers along the barn but couldn't wait for them to bloom. She did a gorgeous job." They wandered to the first fence. "Here we have Nutmeg and Olive. They're both playful and fun and so smart." They rushed to the fence line and let Lydia scratch their heads.

"I love their eyes. They're so big and expressive." Lydia couldn't resist their soft ears either.

"Their neighbors are the two alpacas, Agatha and Arnold. Arnold is a bit shy, so don't take it personally." She walked a few paces ahead past the fence line that separated them from the donkeys. As soon as Olivia put her hand on the fence, Agatha rushed over, and Arnold stayed behind her.

Olivia encouraged Lydia to place her hand out, palm up,

so Agatha could get to know her. It didn't take long for the alpaca to nuzzle Lydia's hand and elicit a giggle. "She sort of tickles," Lydia said. "Aww, Agatha, you're a sweetheart, aren't you?"

"I sure enjoy them, along with the donkeys. And wait until you see the goats and my sweet lamb, Paisley." Olivia motioned her down the pathway toward the bunkhouse.

Olivia opened the gate and led Lydia through it, where the playful goats were romping and frolicking, along with one young lamb. As soon as Paisley saw Olivia, she bolted over to her. Olivia reached down to embrace the lamb, laughing. "Duke says I've ruined her, and she thinks she's a dog."

Lydia petted Paisley's head. "I think he might be right. She's a lovebug, isn't she?"

Olivia patted Paisley's rump and encouraged her to go back to playing. Lydia couldn't get over the herd of goats and their antics. The way they raised up on their back legs and then plopped down with their front ones and climbed onto the wooden spools made her laugh.

"Georgia is a talented seamstress, and she's in the process of making some pajamas for all of them. I can't wait to get them and see how they look."

Lydia's eyes widened. "Oh, those photos will draw people to the farm for sure."

With a nod, Olivia grinned. "That's what Micki said. She wants to put them on our website."

"I'll have to get busy and play with some recipes. Once we find something we like and want to sell, we can take some photos and add them to the website."

"You won't have to twist too many arms to get help sampling treats." Olivia led the way out the gate and back toward the house. She pointed at the door to the shelter.

"I'm going to check on my email and the dogs, and then I'll be in."

"See you in a bit. I need to finish up my laundry, and then we can get started on dinner."

After Lydia made chicken quesadillas with the leftovers they found in the fridge, they settled in to watch some television. With Lydia at one end and Olivia the other, and the dogs piled in the middle of the sofa, they enjoyed a few episodes of a show set in New Zealand, where two people who don't know each other inherit a winery. They laughed and enjoyed the gorgeous scenery.

As they watched, the dogs hurried to the door with Chief and Hope giving a low bark. Vera couldn't help herself and barked several times, and Stubbs joined the choir. Soon after, headlights flashed across the windows. Olivia glanced over at the door where all three golden tails wagged in unison. "Meg must be home."

Moments later, Meg came through the door. She bent down and petted all the dogs and picked up Vera. "She's so cute, I can't help myself." Stubbs couldn't help himself and wiggled closer to her leg.

Lydia smiled at the sight of her tiny ball of fur and her ability to charm everyone. "How was your day?"

"Pretty good," she said with a hint of a smile. "We were busy at the clinic and then went to Rooster's for burgers. Lavender Valley is so quiet, and there's not much to do. Everything closes down pretty early, but we were all tired anyway."

Olivia pointed at the chair. "You can join us if you want."

Meg took a seat and sighed. "I was thinking about going

to the hospital tomorrow to visit my aunt, but it's really hard to just sit there all day. She sleeps most of the time I'm there and still has no memory of me."

Olivia's forehead creased. "You and your mom were just there last night. I don't think it would make any difference if you take a day off and rest tomorrow. People with injuries like hers need rest more than anything. It's how the body heals."

Meg kept petting Vera and lifted Stubbs onto her lap. "Yeah, that make sense. I just feel bad with her being there all alone. I know it's hard on Mom, and I feel guilty sometimes for making her go. Jade was really awful to her."

Olivia welcomed the three goldens back to the middle of the sofa, scratching Willow's head as her eyes closed. "Your mom has years of memories and heartache when it comes to Jade, so just be gentle with her. She needs time, and she's doing her best to help Jade. The nurses will take good care of her and while it's very kind of you to worry about her, she'll be fine resting on her own. Once she's stable enough and more alert, they'll be moving her to a rehab facility. It might be easier to visit her then when she's more apt to be talking and awake."

"I wonder how long that will take?" Meg looked at Olivia with wide eyes.

"It's hard to say. She could wake up tomorrow and remember everything, or it could take months. Her body will get stronger each day, and you'll just have to be patient for her mind to heal. With her injuries, I suspect she'll need at least a month of rehab, maybe longer."

"I wonder where she'll go after that. I'll have to see what Mom thinks."

"Just give it time, Meg. Jade's problems are of her own making, and it's not your job or Micki's to solve them for her. Your mom doesn't need any more pressure when it comes to Jade. I think she's been more than nice and very understanding considering the situation. Try to give your mom the space and time she needs."

Meg nodded. "Yeah, that makes sense.

Lydia wasn't sure what the story was but didn't want to ask. "I could make some popcorn?" Lydia rose from the couch.

Meg nodded. "Okay, that sounds good."

While Lydia used Jewel's old air popcorn machine to make a huge bowl, Olivia got everyone fresh glasses of iced tea. After she dressed and seasoned the popcorn, Lydia poured each of them their own bowl and grabbed a handful of napkins on her way to the living area.

They settled back in to finish their episode and caught Meg up on the gist of the story. After a few bites, Meg looked over at Lydia. "Okay, this is the best popcorn I've had. What did you do to it?"

"Just butter and a tiny bit of cinnamon and sugar." Lydia popped another handful into her mouth.

Meg wasn't all that interested in the show and as soon as she finished her bowl of popcorn, she wiped her hands, put Stubbs on the floor, and placed Vera in Lydia's lap. "I'm going to get to bed. See you guys in the morning."

Before she reached the top step, the dogs darted to the front door and moments later, Harry came through it. "Hey, I wasn't sure you'd both still be up. I hope you weren't waiting for me."

Olivia chuckled. "No, Meg just got in a bit ago, and we were having some popcorn and watching a new show."

"There's popcorn left in the kitchen if you want a bowl." Lydia gestured toward the bowl in her lap.

Olivia took another bite of hers. "Did you and Clay have a nice trip?"

Her smile widened. "It was fun. We drove over to a small town outside of Klamath Falls. It was a nice drive, and Clay checked out a horse one of his clients was interested in buying. It was at a beautiful ranch." She wandered into the kitchen and returned with popcorn and a glass of tea.

Harry sat in the chair, her legs folded, and took her first bite. "Yummy. We had dinner at a cute place. It used to be a hotel, and they remodeled it into a really nice restaurant. Clay knows them because they buy beef from the ranch. It was a great meal."

Olivia gestured toward Harry and waved her hand. "Oh, Lydia, I don't think we had time to tell you, but Harry is the new mayor of Lavender Valley. Did you know that?"

With wide eyes, Lydia turned toward Harry. "I knew you were some kind of chief with the police in Salem." She gave her a sheepish grin. "I did some research and found some newspaper articles with your picture in them, but I didn't check out anything in Lavender Valley. Wow, that's quite an accomplishment."

Harry waved away her praise. "Oh, it's not that big of a deal. I helped break up an amateur criminal enterprise the former mayor was involved with, and the town was so happy, they made me a write-in candidate, and I won." She rolled her eyes. "I wasn't looking for a job, but the more I thought about it, it made sense, and it keeps me busy."

After another swallow from her glass, Olivia glanced over at Lydia. "She's humble. We all think it's impressive. Harry's integrity and honesty, along with her work ethic, was easy for everyone to see. They wanted someone they could trust, and we think it's terrific that our sister is the mayor."

"I guess we better be on our best behavior. Does that

mean we get some get out of jail free cards?" Lydia asked with a chuckle.

Harry shook her head. "Absolutely not. Mostly, it means I'm in lots of meetings, but I'm getting in the groove now and working to streamline things. The previous mayor wasn't doing any actual work for the town, just using her position to line her own pockets, so it's easy to be impressive." She laughed and took another handful of popcorn.

Lydia grinned and said, "I know what you mean. Some of the best jobs I've had were taking over from a bad or lazy chef. Just my normal effort outshines them easily."

Harry nodded. "Thinking about all of us, Jewel's girls, we've all done so well in our careers and excelled. She instilled a strong work ethic in me and always encouraged me to do my best. Olivia rose to the top of her career as a nurse, you're a renowned chef, Micki is a wizard with software, and her company loves her so much, they're willing to let her work from anywhere. Jewel would be so proud."

Olivia jumped up from the couch. "That reminds me, Lydia. You should check out the journals Jewel kept. There's one in the stack with your name on it." She pointed to the shelf in the bookcase.

Harry set aside her bowl. "Not only would Jewel be proud, but she'd also be so happy to see all of us together, under her roof. I think she knew we all needed a family and made sure we'd be here for each other."

Olivia dabbed at her eyes with her napkin. "Sisters. I always wanted a sister, and now I've got the three of you, plus Georgia on her way soon. Like you said, Jewel knew I needed all of you. I'm so thankful to be here."

Tears continued to leak from Olivia's eyes and tugged at Lydia's heart. She handed Olivia a clean napkin. "Are you okay?"

Olivia nodded. "I'm sorry. We all have a story to share, but I'm too tired tonight. When Micki gets home, we'll have to figure out a night to have a sisters' dinner, and maybe Georgia can join us on a video call."

Olivia hugged Lydia and Harry and wished them a good night before padding upstairs. Willow, Stubbs, and Hope followed her.

Harry collected the empty bowls and glasses and on her way back from the kitchen, she yawned. "I think it's time I'm off to bed myself. See you in the morning, Lydia." Chief followed Harry to her bedroom.

Lydia wished her a good night and cradled Vera in her arms, soaking in the fact she was in Jewel's house. After several minutes, she carried Vera out the mudroom door, where she took the path to the motorhome, happy she had her twinkling lights strung across her bedroom on a timer. Once inside, the warm glow lit her way.

Much like the twinkling lights, her new sisters made her world much brighter.

CHAPTER FIVE

Sunday, Lydia woke early, excited to spend time in Jewel's kitchen. Mornings weren't her usual thing, but it had been a long time since she'd had a kitchen to herself for an entire day and could create a meal for friends.

Friends. She hadn't had a circle of friends since she left Portland. Olivia and Harry were so nice and genuine. She felt a strong bond with them already. Although she'd only spent a few minutes with Micki, she longed to know more about her and couldn't wait to share her culinary ideas for the festival with her.

When Harry and Olivia talked about being a family last night, it had stirred something in her. Losing Jewel, even though Lydia wasn't the best at keeping in touch, left Lydia without a family. Jewel and Chuck were the only ones she considered family. She knew she could count on Jewel no matter what. Jewel never gave up on Lydia, despite her wandering and lack of communication.

Her heart ached when she thought about it too much. She wished she would have realized how much she would miss

Jewel when she was gone. She should have made more of an effort to visit her. A tear slipped from her eye and onto her pillow.

As she petted the top of Vera's tiny head, Lydia realized Jewel was still there, guiding her and with her newfound sisters of the heart, giving her a chance at a family. The idea of having a family was exciting and scary. Having people she could count on would be wonderful, but she was scared to get too attached and have to leave.

She never thought too far into the future and vowed to push those worries aside and enjoy each moment she had at the farm. She tossed the blanket off and slid out of bed.

She didn't want to bother Harry this early, so she took a quick shower in her own tiny bathroom. With that done, she collected Vera, who was still stretched out on the bed. She slipped her cell phone into the pocket of her jeans and led Vera outside, where she sniffed at the pathway and clumps of pasture grass along their walk to the house.

Morning sunlight bathed the fields and farmhouse. The beauty and quiet around Lydia made her heart skip a beat. A little part of her wished she could stay on the farm forever. The chances of that happening were slim. The only way she felt safe was to keep moving and not stay in one place too long.

After Vera finished her exploration and completed her business, they went to the mudroom door. She turned the knob, relieved to find it unlocked since she didn't have a key. Vera settled on top of the area rug the dogs used yesterday, and Lydia went about checking her list.

The coffee maker sprang to life and soon, the rich aroma filled the air. Lydia opted to start her dessert first. As quietly as she could, she collected the bowls and pans she would need for her shortcake. Using the old pastry cutter with its wooden handle, she cut the cold butter into her flour mixture and with each flick of her wrist, Lydia smiled. She could almost feel Jewel's hand over hers, guiding it. Jewel had taught her how to use the tool and although Lydia had graduated to using food processors, there was something cathartic about the gentle motion of the pastry cutter.

She could picture Jewel, outfitted in one of her aprons, behind her, reassuring her the dough would come together eventually.

In no time, she had the dough ready to go into the oven and slipped the pan inside, setting the timer for fifteen minutes. While it cooked, she washed and rinsed the bowl and utensils. She had to wait until closer to serving time to prepare the strawberries and fresh whipped cream. She didn't want the berries to release their juices early.

While the shortbread baked, she took out the top round roast from the refrigerator and selected a sharp knife from the block on the counter. She caught the timer before it sounded and checked the shortbread, opting to give it another minute or two.

When it was the perfect golden brown, she removed it and set it aside to cool. Lydia was a huge fan of slab pies and intended to do the same thing with a fresh strawberry shortcake.

She gathered a few more ingredients and put together a filling made with parmesan cheese, breadcrumbs, minced garlic, and fresh basil from Micki's herb garden. She stirred it together and closed her eyes as she breathed in the lovely aroma. She sprinkled in salt and pepper and gave it another stir before tackling the roast waiting for her. With deft movements, she used the knife to carve thin slices of meat and set them on parchment paper.

As she was finishing, Harry and Olivia, along with the

three goldens and Stubbs, came from around the corner. "Something smells delicious," said Olivia, eyeing the granite counter covered with meat slices.

Harry made a beeline from the coffee maker and retrieved three cups. "Everybody want coffee this morning?"

Olivia nodded. "Sounds great. I'm going to feed the dogs but will be right there."

Lydia glanced behind her. "I think I'll hold off until I get this part done, then I'll join you."

With the dogs fed, Olivia and Harry sat at the counter, sipping coffee, while they watched Lydia work.

After a trip to the refrigerator for the prosciutto, Lydia placed a thin slice atop each piece of beef and then added the filling over it. Once they were all prepared, she rolled up the slices, tucking in the ends and then securing the roll with toothpicks.

Harry's eyes widened as she watched. "I'm fascinated by all this. What are you making?"

Lydia glanced up as she finished rolling the beef slices. "It's an Italian dish called beef braciole. It basically means stuffed and cooked in sauce."

Olivia looked over at Harry. "I'm totally impressed already and haven't even had a bite."

Lydia laughed and added olive oil to a pot on the cooktop. Using tongs, she placed the rolls in the pan, seam side down and let them brown.

Harry shook her head. "You're killing me now. The smell of that is making me so hungry." She turned to Olivia. "We're going to have to smell that all day and wait until dinner. I don't know if I can do it."

Olivia added more coffee to her cup. "We should probably eat some breakfast. I think we've got some oatmeal that would be quick."

Harry turned up her nose. "I'm going to run to the Sugar Shack. Any special requests?"

Lydia raised her brows. "I remember their cinnamon rolls. How about one of those for me?"

Olivia grinned. "Croissant for me, but I'll eat anything."

Harry nodded and collected her purse. "Got it. I'll be back in a flash. Do you need anything else from the market?"

Lydia shook her head. "Since you're going to the bakery, could you pick up some fresh bread? I want to make garlic bread out of it." She gasped and then added, "I do need a key to the house. I realized that this morning and was glad I forgot to lock the mudroom door."

Harry offered to take the dogs for a ride, and they jumped at the chance. "I'll stop by and get a couple made. Georgia will need one, too." She looked down at Vera and Stubbs, who stood at the door with the big dogs. "Can Vera and Stubbs come with us?"

Lydia laughed. "Sure."

Olivia nodded and collected their leashes. She helped Harry attach them and watched as Harry led them to her SUV. She put the three goldens in the back and added Vera and Stubbs to the passenger seat. Olivia and Lydia watched from the window, smiling at the car full of dogs as Harry headed down the driveway.

"Harry never had a dog until she adopted Chief from her old partner who passed away. I think she's becoming a dog person." Olivia went back to her chair at the counter. "Those dogs never miss a chance for a trip. They're always up for an adventure."

Lydia nodded as she put the browned rolls on a plate. She reached for a half bottle of red wine she found in the fridge. "Hope it's okay to use this up?"

Olivia nodded. "Oh, yes. It's from Clay and Heath and needs to be used."

Lydia removed the cork and sniffed the bottle. "It smells so good." She fingered the label. "Clay and Heath have good taste in wine."

"Wait until you see their house. It's got a huge wine cellar, among many other gorgeous amenities."

Lydia poured the wine into the pot, and it sizzled, deglazing the pan. She added in slices of garlic and stirred it, making sure all the bits of beef were incorporated in the liquid. After adding in broth, crushed tomatoes, and seasonings, she stirred it and let it simmer.

Olivia sniffed in the aroma. "That smells so good."

Lydia moved the two slow cookers she found in the cupboards and set them on the counter. "I'm going to finish these in the slow cooker. I think they're much better when cooked slowly all day."

She poured the sauce into the slow cookers and then added in the browned beef rolls, making sure to cover them in the sauce. She topped them with lids and set them to cook on low.

As she and Olivia were doing the dishes, Harry returned with her band of merry canines. She placed a pink bakery box on the counter and unleashed her furry companions.

Harry handed Olivia the leashes and hurried to the door. "I'll grab the bread, and I stopped and got us lattes, too."

With the kitchen clean and the beef rolls cooking, Lydia settled into a chair at the counter and plucked a cinnamon roll from the box. Moments later, Harry returned with chai tea lattes for everyone, including one for Meg.

As soon as Harry and Olivia sat with their plates, Meg came down the stairs, her hair wet from a shower. Harry gestured to the box of pastries and pointed at the cup. "I brought you a latte."

Meg slipped an arm around Harry's shoulders. "You're the best, Aunt Harry. Can I call you Aunt Harry?"

Harry laughed and reached for her cup. "Sure, you can. You've got three new aunts, and another one who will be here soon."

"I told Mom I'd always wanted a bigger family. I guess my wish came true." She grinned at all of them and selected a croissant from the box. "So, you guys think Buck is a good guy, right? I think Mom really likes him, and I never remember her going on a date the whole time I lived at home."

Harry nodded. "Buck is a great guy. He's honest and hardworking and a pillar of the community. I think he's also quite smitten with your mom."

Meg wrinkled her nose. "Smitten. How old are you, Harry?"

Olivia laughed and said, "Younger than me, but I agree. Buck is kind and respected and well, just wonderful. He's also besotted with your mom. How's that? Even more old school than smitten."

Meg laughed. "You guys are so funny. Yeah, I think he's totally legit. I just don't want to see Mom hurt."

Olivia shook her head. "I know he wouldn't do that. He's a very serious guy, not one to enter into dating or a relationship lightly. Duke's sister told me how everyone is so pleased to see him so happy. He's a workaholic and a homebody. He's not a player."

Harry took another sip of her latte. "I think your mom poured her heart and soul into raising you and your brother. When your dad died, her entire focus shifted to working hard to give both of you a good life. I'd say her chance at happiness is long overdue and from seeing how excited she was to go on this getaway, I think Buck is the reason she's so happy."

Meg finished her croissant and ran her finger through the powdered sugar on her plate. "You're right about her working so hard. I guess at the time, I didn't really notice. I want her to be happy and as upset as I was with her this past year, I don't want her to be alone or sad."

Olivia looked between Harry and Lydia. They both shrugged, and Olivia turned to Meg. "Speaking as a mom, it's hard to let your kids go, especially when they've been the center of your universe and your whole focus. Micki has great judgment, and I think she's given you your space to live on your own away at college, right?"

Meg nodded, her hands around her cup.

"She deserves the same freedom and grace to find her new path now that you and your brother are out of the house. It's an adjustment, and she's finding her way. I know she loves you more than life itself." A tear fell from Olivia's eye, and she flicked it away with her finger.

Meg rose from her chair and engulfed Olivia in a hug. "I'm sorry, Aunt Olivia. I'm sure you're thinking of your son." She hugged her tighter, and they held each other for a few minutes.

Olivia reached up and patted Meg's hand. "You're such a kindhearted young lady. I'm so happy to be Aunt Olivia."

Meg released her and walked over to Lydia. "Whatever you're making smells so good. I can't wait for dinner. If you're Aunt Lydia, I guess that makes Vera my cousin, right?" Meg giggled and smiled at Lydia.

"I've never been an aunt, so that's exciting, and I'm thrilled you're my new niece. Like you, I always wished for a bigger family with aunts and cousins. Outside of the dogs

Jewel had when I was here, Vera's my first dog. She's my first pet of any kind."

"She's a total heartthrob," said Meg, looking over at her resting on the rug with the big dogs and Stubbs. "I think I might take them all for a walk down to the creek. Is that okay?"

Olivia's eyes brightened. "That sounds like a great idea; I'll go with you. Lydia doesn't need us hovering over her while she creates her masterpiece."

Harry finished her latte and slipped out of her chair. "I could use a walk, especially after that cinnamon roll. I need to up my exercise. I might have to take Chief to work a few days a week, so I have a good excuse to go walking."

"Dogs are definitely a motivator when it comes to exercise. I think I'll take Milton and Thelma with us. With all of us, if the small dogs get too tired, we can carry them."

The three of them collected water bottles and sunglasses, and Lydia gave Vera a gentle pat on the head on her way out the door. "You be a good girl." She stood at the window and smiled as she watched them take to the trail with the little dogs hurrying to keep up with the goldens.

Lydia followed them outside and dashed through Gypsy's door. With a full day of cooking, she wouldn't have time to focus on her appearance but wanted to make a good impression on their guests. She put on a blue shirt with purple hues that brought out her eyes, put her now-dry hair into a quick updo that kept it out of her face and off her neck. She added a bit of makeup and mascara, along with some earrings and the cross necklace the ladies had given her.

She pronounced it as good as it would get and hurried back to the house, where she donned an apron to protect her shirt. With her heart filled and loving the idea of being an aunt, she turned her attention to the prep work.

Lydia retrieved the radio Jewel always kept in the mudroom and tuned it to a station that came in the clearest. Country music filled the air as she donned an apron and checked her list. First, she put together the pizza dough for the appetizer she planned. She used the fancy stand mixer Jewel loved and combined the ingredients into dough. She loved to knead by hand and opted to use her hands to push and pull the dough. She put it in an oiled bowl and covered it with a towel to let it rise.

Next, Lydia prepared the balsamic poppyseed dressing she needed for her strawberry spinach salad. After a taste of it to make sure it was perfect, she added pecans to a baking sheet and toasted them in the oven before chopping them for the salad.

She sliced red onions and put them in a bowl of cold water and then retrieved the strawberries and sliced them. While she was in the slicing mood, she worked on the mushrooms and set them aside. The risotto she was planning wouldn't take long to cook, but she wanted to get as much of the prep done as possible.

After hunting through Jewel's cabinets, she found a glass bowl with a lid and went about adding the fresh baby spinach to the bowl, along with rings of red onion she chopped into smaller pieces. She added the strawberries, pieces of goat cheese, and the toasted pecans. Before sealing it with the lid, she couldn't resist a bite. A chef always tests her dishes.

She tucked it into the fridge to await the dressing when it was time to serve it.

While she waited for the dough, she gathered the

ingredients for garlic butter. As she prepared to chop the fresh parsley, her phone chimed.

Her heartbeat quickened as she pulled the phone from her pocket. She relaxed when she saw a text from Olivia. They had run into Heath and Clay on their way back from the creek, and they invited them to stop by the ranch for refreshments. Olivia wanted to know if she could join them.

She texted back a quick reply and let her know she was knee-deep in cooking, but she asked if they might bring some wine to go with dinner. She had totally spaced on that when she was shopping, concentrating on the food.

Olivia sent back a smiley face and assured her they would handle the wine.

Lydia was in the middle of slicing the bread when the sound of footsteps on the porch startled her. She'd been engrossed in her cooking and wasn't even sure the door was locked. She adjusted her grip on the knife.

CHAPTER SIX

She kept hold of the knife and walked over to the window, keeping to the side to stay out of view. She spotted a dark-haired man she'd never seen, reaching into the trunk of a car. Her pulse quickened, and she slipped the cell phone from her pocket.

Micki came from the other side of the car and embraced the man. Lydia let out a long breath. He put his arm around her and toted a bag on his shoulder.

Lydia slid her phone back in her pocket and hurried to her place behind the granite counter to finish slicing the loaves of bread. She took several slow breaths, willing her pulse to slow.

Micki came through the door with her bag, a bouquet of gorgeous flowers, and a happy smile. She caught Lydia's eye. "Oh, something smells yummy." She looked around and toward the living area. "Where is everybody?"

Her comment about the smell from the slow cookers prompted Lydia to check on her beef rolls. She looked through the glass lids, satisfied that the sauce covered the rolls and that it looked like it was thickening nicely.

Micki collected the empty vase from the dining room table and filled it with water before she added the stems of peonies and roses, along with lemon leaf. She placed it in the center of the table and admired it.

"They all took the dogs for a walk to the creek and then ran into Heath and Clay, so they're over at their place taking a break. I think they were trying to stay out of my way while I was cooking. They're also bringing wine for dinner."

Micki pointed back at the front door, and the man with the dark hair came from around the corner, carrying two tote bags. "Buck and I bought some wine at the Dragonfly Estate and wanted to share it with everyone, too." Micki laughed and said, "Oh, I'm sorry. You haven't even met Buck yet. Buck Simpson, this is Lydia Morrow."

Lydia extended her hand across the counter. "Happy to meet you. I recognize your name from Harry's letter. I've already had the pleasure of meeting Stubbs."

He shook her hand and smiled. "Stubbs is a charmer. Micki told me you arrived, and I'm so glad you're here. Harry was going to begin an exhaustive search for you next week."

Lydia chuckled. "I guess I showed up just in time then." She gestured to the chairs at the counter. "Come sit down and tell me about your trip."

Micki stashed a couple of bottles of wine in the fridge and went about putting the other bottles in a cupboard. "The trip was fabulous," she said, reaching for glasses and pouring iced teas for all three of them. "The estate is beyond beautiful, and the food was delicious."

Buck put his hands on the back of one of the chairs. "Are

you sure we aren't going to be in your way while you're cooking?"

Lydia shook her head as she finished coating the bread with garlic butter and wrapped it in foil. "Not at all. I'm going to make the appetizer soon and then just have a few things to finish off right before we're ready to eat."

After a long swallow from her glass, Micki met Lydia's eyes. "How was Meg while I was gone?"

She grinned as she sprinkled flour on the counter and rolling pin. "She's taken to calling me Aunt Lydia. Same with Harry and Olivia. She talked quite a bit about your sister in the hospital."

The smile disappeared from Micki's face. "Jade. That's a long story."

With a shrug of her shoulders, Lydia rolled out the dough. "I've got time."

After a reassuring squeeze of her hand from Buck, Micki took a deep breath. "Jade is my older sister, and I haven't seen her or my mother since I came to Jewel's. My mother died long ago, and I never told my late husband or my children about Jade or the abuse I suffered. For school projects that required family information, I just simply said my parents were dead, and I had no other relatives."

Lydia placed the pizza crust on a pan and started on the second ball of dough.

"Meg's been away at college in Colorado. She was invited there and left the University of Washington last year to try out Colorado State. Jade ran into her at an animal clinic she was working at for school, and Jade thought she looked like me and struck up a friendship. Meg asked me if I had a sister, and I denied it, which was a mistake."

She took another sip from her glass. "Anyway, it created a huge rift between us, and Meg refused my calls and texts. It was awful and broke my heart." She blinked away the tears in her eyes. "In the process, she told Jade I had moved here, and she showed up at the farm. Along with her general nastiness, she kept coming back and wanted money to leave Meg alone. Knowing it was a mistake, but hoping to buy time to convince Meg what Jade was really like, I paid her. She came back for more and with Harry and Olivia urging me on, I elicited help from Buck, and we got a restraining order."

Lydia arched her brows. "Wow, that's horrible."

"It gets worse." Micki rolled her eyes. "We were all set for a hearing where the judge would allow Jade to explain her side of the story for a permanent restraining order when Jade hit a tree, totaled her old car, and ended up in the hospital with some serious injuries. When she woke up a few days ago, she didn't know us or remember anything."

After placing the second pizza round on the pan, Lydia went about doing the dishes and wiping down the counter.

Buck cleared his throat. "We ended up having to go back to court to withdraw the restraining order since legally, Micki and Meg were prohibited from contact with Jade. Micki wanted to try to help her and do what she could. It's complicated since Jade is on Medicaid in Colorado, so they're working to get her enrolled in Oregon."

With a swipe of a clean towel, Lydia dried the counter. "Olivia talked to Meg quite a bit when she brought up Jade last night. She thinks she'll be in rehab for at least a month and thought it would be easier for Meg to visit her when she was more alert. I can see why Olivia was such a great nurse. She's calm and assured Meg that Jade would be just fine without someone at her bedside each day."

Micki sighed. "Yes, it's hard for me to go and sit with her. Although, since she doesn't remember anything, it's easier. I want to try to help her, but she's not a good person, and I'm having a difficult time putting aside all the pain she caused me in the past and more recently by manipulating Meg and extorting money from me. It's a bad situation."

Buck reached for her hand and smiled. "That's one reason I thought Micki deserved a getaway this weekend."

She leaned her head closer to his. "It was exactly what I needed."

"I'm sorry you're going through all of that," said Lydia, taking two lemons from the fridge. "Meg has a soft heart, I can tell. I think she's torn between her love for you and trying to help Jade."

Micki nodded. "It's going to get more complicated, I'm sure. Once Jade's released, I don't know what will happen. I just know she can't come here. I'm willing to help her get on her feet, but I can't be around her constantly."

Lydia checked the time. "Yeah, I don't blame you there. I don't have siblings, that I know of." She chuckled and added, "I'm not sure I could be as gracious as you." She eyed the dining room table. "Would you two be willing to set the table? I suspect they'll be showing up soon. I'll get these pizzas in the oven and ready for snacking while I finish the rest of the meal."

Micki slid from her chair. "We're on it." She went to the cupboards and pulled out placemats and plates and handed them to Buck.

While they worked on the table, Lydia brushed the crusts with olive oil and added mozzarella cheese and parmesan. In the midst of her doing that, everyone arrived and came through the door.

Micki was busy hugging Meg, Buck knelt to welcome Stubbs, and Olivia herded the dogs away from the dining room. As Lydia turned from slipping the pizza crusts into the oven, she noticed Harry coming around the corner.

She held the hand of a man wearing a dark-brown cowboy hat. "Lydia, this is Clay Nolan."

He removed his hat, revealing sandy-blond hair and smiling blue eyes. He extended his hand. "It's great to meet you, Lydia." He glanced around the kitchen and added, "Whatever you're making smells terrific."

Lydia wiped her hands on her apron and shook his hand. "Wonderful to meet you, and I hope you think the same once you taste dinner. I'll have our appetizer ready in a few minutes."

He gestured behind him. "Heath is bringing in some wine. He's the cook in our family, so I'm sure he'll be talking your ear off."

Harry retrieved a pitcher of water and filled the glasses on the table, while Micki added wine glasses to each place setting. As she refilled the pitcher, she smiled over at Lydia. "This is the first big dinner party we've had. Everything looks wonderful." At the sound of the front door opening, Harry's eyes glanced toward it. "Here's Heath now."

Moments later, another man, this one wearing a black cowboy hat, came from around the corner. He held a cloth bag filled with bottles of wine. He stepped forward to the counter, set the bag down, and removed his hat.

Lydia stifled a gasp. It was blue eyes from the farmer's market.

He grinned at her and extended his hand. "We meet again. I'm Heath."

She stared at his striking blue eyes, unable to find any words as she held onto his hand.

CHAPTER SEVEN

"Again?" asked Clay. "Where did you two meet?"

Heath let go of her hand and chuckled. "Farmer's market. We ran into each other, so to speak."

His easy grin made Lydia's heart beat faster. She reached for her glass of tea, now mostly melted water from the ice, and took a long swallow. "Heath's being kind. I wasn't watching where I was going and stumbled right into the back of him." She stammered, "I didn't know who he was."

Heath raised his nose in the air. "Something smells beyond delicious. I can't wait to eat whatever it is you've prepared. Jewel always talked about your accomplishments. I seem to remember you won that baking contest on television, right?"

Lydia's cheeks bloomed. She waved her hand in front of her. "Oh, that was a long time ago. I just hope I don't disappoint you."

The timer buzzed on the oven and when she turned back around with the pizzas, Heath was the only one in the room.

He was unpacking the wine and took out a few bottles of beer, opening one of them and putting the rest in the fridge.

She went about adding the fresh arugula to the top of the pizzas. She squeezed lemon juice over them and sprinkled them with salt and pepper before cutting them into wedges.

The dogs rushing to the front door announced another guest. Olivia hurried to open it for a handsome man, who greeted her with a hug. Heath caught Lydia's eye. "That's Duke Walker, the local veterinarian. He's a great guy, and he and Olivia have hit it off."

She wiped her hands on a towel and put out a serving spatula next to the pizzas and the appetizer plates. "Would you mind letting them know the appetizer is ready?" Lydia walked over to the cooktop. "I need to start the risotto."

He took a quick sip from his bottle. "Don't start without me. I want to help."

It didn't take long for the rest of them to pile into the kitchen and help themselves to slices of the arugula pizza, which they all raved about. Olivia and Duke came in through the mudroom door.

She made her way to Lydia and placed her hand on his shoulder. "I wanted to formally introduce you to Duke Walker. This is our new sister, Lydia Morrow." She waved her hand over the counter. "As you can see, she's a talented chef."

Duke shook Lydia's hand. "It's wonderful to meet you. We're all so glad you're here."

Olivia pointed at the door. "Duke and I fed all the dogs and left them to lounge in the shelter. We've got quite the crowd tonight and don't need them underfoot. I left Vera in one of the stables with Hope, so she can't wander around and get into anything."

Lydia smiled at both of them. "It's a pleasure to meet you,

Duke. I've heard so many good things about you from Meg and Olivia and everyone. Thanks for taking care of Vera." She pointed at the pizza. "Grab a slice of our appetizer, and I'll have dinner on the table soon."

She left them to help themselves and returned to the cooktop. Heath was already putting on an apron when she added olive oil to the sauté pan. He washed his hands and held them out. "How can I help?"

Lydia had him retrieve the sliced mushrooms, chopped onion, and cheese from the fridge, along with wine and broth. He toted all of it to the counter next to her. "I can grab the arborio rice, just point me to it."

She arched her brows. "Wow, I'm impressed. Clay told me you were the chef of the family." She nodded toward a cupboard, and he brought her the rice.

"Mushroom risotto is one of my favorite things to make," he said, eyeing the mushrooms sautéing in the pan.

She removed them, turned down the heat, and added butter. As soon as it melted, Heath was ready to dump in the onions. She added salt, stirred, and let them soften before stirring in the rice. She asked Heath to add in the white wine.

He poured, and she stirred as the sauce simmered. "Once this is reduced, we'll just add in the broth one cup at a time. Doing it slowly makes it creamier."

Heath leaned over and looked in the pan, inhaling the scent. "That smells good, and I didn't know that about the broth. I'll try that next time."

She left him in charge of adding the broth and filled a pot with water to boil while she opened the package of capellini. She retrieved the salad and dressed it and popped the garlic bread into the oven. She came up behind Heath to check his progress. "That looks great."

"What are you making? I smell roasting beef and some kind of tomato sauce, maybe even bacon."

Her eyes sparkled with mystery. "You've got a good nose on ya." She chuckled and checked her pot of boiling water before she reached for a large platter. After checking on the risotto and adding in the sautéed mushrooms, parmesan, a dash of white wine vinegar, and the truffle oil, she reduced the heat and asked Heath to stir it while she added the pasta to the boiling water.

"Okay, another secret," he said, smiling as he stirred. "That little dash of vinegar." He tapped his forehead. "I've got it stored up here for next time."

She handed him a serving bowl and waited a few more minutes for the pasta, which she drained and buttered before adding it to the serving platter. With that done, she quickly added the beef rolls and sauce from one of the crockpots.

Heath put the warm garlic bread in a basket, added the bowl of risotto to the table, and hollered for everyone to come to eat. He carried the huge platter of beef braciole to the table and took a seat, leaving the one next to him open for Lydia.

Soon, all nine of them gathered around Jewel's big dining room table. Micki's flowers set off the beautiful table. Clay was sitting closest to the platter of braciole and offered to dish it up for everyone, since it was too large to pass.

He kept busy, while everyone passed the risotto, salad, and bread around the table. Micki looked down at her plate and smiled across the table at Lydia. "This looks marvelous. I bet you could get a job at the Dragonfly. It looks just as good as what they served last night."

As he added a heaping spoonful of risotto to his plate, he nodded. "Oh, yeah, this looks and smells amazing."

Clay's job was finally done, and he settled into his seat.

Then, Harry picked up her glass of wine. "A toast to the chef. Thank you, Lydia, for this wonderful meal. We should be welcoming you, but it seems you've turned the tables and worked to welcome us. I know I speak for all of us when I say we're so glad you're back at the farm with your sisters of the heart."

Everyone clinked glasses or beer bottles, in the case of Heath and Clay, and echoed Harry's words. Then, they dug into the meal. Moans of delight resonated around the table. "This sauce is epic," said Meg, taking another bite of the main dish.

Clay caught his brother's eye. "I thought you made the best mushroom risotto, but I think she's got you beat."

Heath laughed. "I would agree, but hanging out in the kitchen, I learned her secret." He winked at her and made her blush.

Her heart warmed and for the first time in a long time, she felt like part of something good. "You're all so kind," she said, taking a forkful of salad. "I'm so pleased you like it. It's my idea of comfort food, perfect for Sunday dinner."

Around the table, the conversation was easy, relaxed, and full of laughter. Olivia reached for another helping of salad. "This is so yummy. I ate a ton of salads for lunch when I was working, and this tops them all."

"I can make it again and add chicken. It makes a great lunch." Lydia beamed as everyone continued heaping on compliments.

Clay finished his last bite of the braciole and caught Heath's eye. "You know, you ought to invite Lydia to the chili cookoff this week."

Heath nodded as he finished chewing. "There's a big rodeo in town, and they host a chili cookoff. You should enter."

Duke chuckled. "Heath has won that contest every year for how long now?"

He grinned and said, "Five years, but who's counting?"

Buck reached for his glass of water. "What do you say, Lydia? Think you can dethrone the King of Chili?"

Clay grinned at Heath. "Please, Lydia. He's insufferable, and we don't need another chili trophy."

"It sounds fun," said Lydia. "But I doubt I'll win. I haven't made chili in a long time."

"Whew," said Heath with a wide grin. "Maybe I'll have a fighting chance."

As everyone finished and pronounced the meal delicious, Lydia gestured back toward the kitchen. "I've got a slab strawberry shortcake for dessert, but I still need to whip the cream and slice the berries. It needs to be fresh when it's served."

Harry rose from her chair. "Why don't you take a well-deserved break while we do the dishes and clean up the kitchen. I don't think we'll be ready for dessert until much later."

Everyone nodded, patting their bellies and agreeing they were stuffed. Meg, Clay, Heath, and Harry took charge of dish duty, and Micki suggested she take Lydia on a walk through the garden and flowers. They tugged on their boots, and Olivia and Duke went to check on the dogs.

Buck joined Micki, and they held hands as they walked along the pathway to the lavender fields. She pointed out the fresh green growth on the healthy plants, some with the beginnings of tiny buds. Micki touched the soft growth and grinned. "I can't wait until we see the first flowers."

Bees buzzed among the plants, ignoring them, and focused only on the lavender. "It's so peaceful and pretty," said Lydia. "I can't wait to see it."

Micki explained about the local beekeeper placing hives and let her know where they were, so she'd steer clear of them. She walked over to the new field, where her dahlias were growing. "I just planted these after I arrived. I'm hoping to lengthen our season at the farm. These dahlias will bloom later, after the lavender, and take us into fall."

Lydia studied the field with the stakes and string running across the rows. Micki explained the stems would need to be staked as the dahlias grew, so the stakes and strings made it easy to do that. Lydia wandered along the edge, admiring the work. "I love dahlias and all their varieties of color and types of flowers. I remember seeing some that were huge."

"They are fabulous. I bought these tubers from an Oregon grower. They're the best."

She and Lydia continued their walk at a slow pace. "Olivia and I were chatting, and I thought it would be fun to make dog treats. I used to do that with Jewel. We might be able to sell them at the festival. I know we could sell some cookies and other treats. I've got some ideas to try out."

"Oh, that would be wonderful. Yes to all of that. They probably told you I'm trying to expand our income streams with some lavender products for retail. That reminds me I need to get you some samples to try."

"I'd love that. I used some of the scrub in Harry's shower, and it was great."

"Back to your idea on cookies and treats, you probably need some sort of license for food, right?"

"If I'm only doing baked goods, nothing that includes meat or needs refrigeration, I can do it without being approved. Just need a food safety class, which I already have."

Micki's smile widened. "Even better news. I love the idea and would love to add some photos to the website."

"I'll get to work on some ideas this week so we can taste

test them. We can't sell them online without having a true business and commercial kitchen, but we can sell them during the festival. It might be fun to experiment with some cookie art. Maybe some dahlia cookies?"

Micki linked her arm in Lydia's. "That would be fantastic. Sort of like my sunflower mural."

They kept walking back to the house and came in through the mudroom and slipped off their boots. They found the kitchen clean and sparkling, the dogs stretched out on the area rug, and everyone gathered on the couch and sofa.

Dessert plates were waiting on the counter, along with the leftover bottles of wine. Lydia donned an apron and gathered the strawberries. She rinsed them in a colander and sliced them. As she added a cutting board full of them to a bowl, Heath came from around the corner. "Want some help?"

"Sure," she said, getting another cutting board and knife for him.

He washed his hands and began the task of slicing. After she added another cutting board full to the bowl, she reached for the carton of cream and added it to the stand mixer.

"Oh," she said. "I meant to ask you about the Ranch House. May said you or Clay might be able to introduce me to the owners. I need to earn some money and prefer working at an actual restaurant. She said they're the most upscale one in town."

He finished slicing a berry. "Yes, it's a great place, and I'd be happy to introduce you, especially now that I've had the true delight of eating one of your meals. How about we go there this week for dinner? My treat."

Part of her wondered if he was asking her on a date, but she didn't care. She needed to find a job. The sooner, the better. She wasn't above using a connection to get an introduction. That was often how the world worked. "I hate to have you buy dinner. We could just stop by."

He shook his head. "I insist. Plus, it'll give you a chance to sample their fare before you talk to Cheryl and Cyrus. They moved here from Seattle with a dream to have a restaurant. They do a great job, grow lots of their own food and most importantly, they buy all their beef from us." He winked at her and chuckled.

"Okay, then. It's a date." She started to clarify what she meant, but instead, turned on the motor, and the machine whirred to life, whipping through the heavy cream. She watched the cream spin, adding in part of the powdered sugar and waiting for it to incorporate.

That same little part of her that wondered if it was a date, wished it might be. There was a warmth about Heath, and she was drawn not only to his stunning eyes, but to his humor and love of food. The idea of dinner with him sparked something deep inside her.

She, however, was a horrible judge when it came to men. She had learned her lesson and steered clear of any hint of a relationship.

She resolved to keep things professional, but when she glanced over to check on his progress with the berries, she couldn't help but see the grin on Heath's face.

CHAPTER EIGHT

Tuesday, after spending the day experimenting with a few cookie combinations, which she left on a plate so Olivia, Harry, and Micki could sample them, Lydia took a shower in Harry's bathroom to get ready for her dinner with Heath. Her wardrobe didn't offer many choices, but she opted for her newest pair of jeans and a lightweight shirt in a blue print that reminded her of a mandala or even a dahlia. It had a flattering V-neck and a bit of a flutter in the elbow-length sleeves.

It looked fancier than a plain old T-shirt but was just as comfy. She took the time to dry her hair and add in a few beach waves with a curling iron. It had been a long time since she'd worn it down and styled it. Someone once told her she had the perfect hair for a California girl. After a quick application of foundation and blush, she swiped her eyes with mascara and added a shimmer of gloss across her lips.

She added the silver cross, which hung perfectly in the center of the opening at her neck. She slipped into a pair of sandals. She glanced down at her toes and realized she needed to give herself a pedicure. She didn't have time for that.

Instead, she climbed over the tub and sat on the edge, rolled up the legs of her jeans, and gave them a quick working over with the lavender salt scrub. Her nails still didn't look great, but at least her feet were smooth and felt good.

She toweled them dry and slipped them back into her sandals. She was tempted to trek back to the motorhome to find a pair of clogs but decided if anyone judged her by her toes, she didn't want to be around them anyway.

She collected her dirty clothes and added them to the laundry basket in the mudroom. The house was quiet. Harry was having dinner with Clay at the ranch, and Olivia and Duke were eating with his family. Harry offered to take the dogs with her and assured Lydia she'd watch over Vera and introduce her to the neighbor dogs. Having taken off the weekend and Monday, Micki took Meg to visit Jade at the hospital in Medford.

She checked the time and opted for a splash of wine. The bottle of white she used for the risotto was delicious and needed to be finished. Despite her offering to meet Heath at the restaurant, he insisted he would pick her up and drive them to town. She added a bit more than a splash to a glass and left the bottle empty. She wasn't driving, so why not take advantage of it?

With the first swallow, she willed it to calm her nerves. After listening to the others talk about the wonderful meals at the Ranch House over dessert on Sunday, she really wanted to impress them and land a job in their kitchen.

She fingered the file folder next to her purse. Micki had been kind enough to take the time to help Lydia prepare a resume yesterday. She hadn't had to use one in years, instead landing most of her jobs via interview, recommendation, or preparing a dish or two, or like at the Burger Barn, by answering an advertisement.

Micki told her how impressive her credentials were and assured her she would have no problem getting a position. Her kind words helped boost Lydia's confidence, which was perpetually low.

She looked over the resumé one more time and finished her wine. As she was rinsing the glass, she heard the chime of the front gate. She dried the glass, put it away, took the folder and her handbag, and hurried out the door.

She was just coming down the porch steps when Heath pulled in and rushed over to open the passenger door of his truck. Relieved to see he was wearing jeans too, she returned his slow smile. He'd chosen a deep-blue shirt that brought out his almost electric-blue eyes.

After shutting her door, he climbed behind the wheel and glanced over at her. "You look really nice, Lydia."

She rubbed her fingers along the corner of the file folder. "Thanks, I'm sort of nervous."

His forehead creased. "Aw, don't be. You're a fabulous chef. I stopped by and talked to Cyrus and Cheryl yesterday and told them about you and the wonderful meal you made. They're excited to meet you."

She nodded and let out a long breath. "So, the ice has been broken?"

"Exactly. I told them we were coming in for dinner tonight and that you had grown up here, and you're looking for work."

"Thanks, Heath. I truly appreciate you doing that."

"They'd be lucky to have you. I think you'd fit right in with their style. They love using local ingredients and always have a few special entrees in addition to their regular menu. I think your creativity could shine there."

He pulled into a parking spot. His words boosted her spirits, and she took the hand he offered her as he held the truck door open for her. Hanging baskets and pots filled with red and purple flowers greeted them as they made their way up the porch steps. Lydia walked through the front door and took in the ambience, which fit with the exterior Victorian theme. Lots of tufted velvet furniture and wood gave it an authentic feel. To the right of the entrance was a large wooden bar with thick cushioned wooden-backed stools. A huge rack of glass and stemware hung over the bartender, and the mirror behind her reflected the room.

The lounge was filled with small tables, velvet chairs, and settees, a few wing-backed chairs and although not lit, a fireplace. The stamped copper ceiling, with thick beams running across it, gave the space a homey feel. Lydia scanned the board on the wall showcasing the specials for the evening. A couple of steaks along with salmon were among the offerings.

A woman with dark hair hurried over to the hostess station. "Heath, I'm so glad to see you." She moved toward him and hugged him. She turned to Lydia. "You must be the chef he's told us so much about. I'm Cheryl Levine. My husband Cyrus is in the kitchen but wants to meet you."

Lydia shook her hand. "Wonderful to meet you. I'm Lydia Morrow. Your restaurant is beautiful, and I've heard fabulous things about your food. Heath tells me you grow some of your own vegetables."

She chuckled, throwing her head back. "We do in the winter but take advantage of all the lovely local produce during the growing season. Cyrus has a greenhouse, so we grow what we can, and I do think it sets us apart."

She motioned to them to follow her. "We've got you set up at a table." She led them through the lounge to a room on the other side of the fireplace. The moment they were seated, a staff member arrived with glasses of water, fresh bread, butter, and dipping oil.

Cheryl handed them menus and reminded them about the specials. They opted to stick with water and passed on the offer of cocktails. "I'll give you a few minutes and as soon as Cyrus can get out of the kitchen, we'll stop by and chat with you."

After a few minutes of perusing the menu, Lydia was satisfied she would have no problem preparing any of the dishes. The menu wasn't huge, which was a relief. They had a smattering of appetizers, steaks, seafood, poultry, limited side dishes, and a few desserts.

Lydia decided on the chardonnay chicken, and Heath selected the rib eye finished with a rosemary and black truffle butter. He opted for tomato bisque soup, and Lydia chose the house salad.

The server left them to nibble on the warm bread, which Lydia pronounced delicious. Lydia glanced around the room, noting the other two tables were empty. "It's quiet in here tonight."

Heath nodded as he tore off a piece of bread to dip. "Weekdays are slower, but there are several more rooms throughout, and they may have people in them. I think Cheryl thought she was doing us a favor to put us in this more intimate room."

"It's lovely. All the antiques and the furnishings embrace the Victorian era." She noticed the bookcases that flanked the fireplace. "It's almost like eating in someone's home."

Their starters arrived, and Lydia took a bite of the crisp salad with a poppyseed dressing. Heath moved the plate with his soup bowl on it toward the center of the table. "Do you want to try this? I thought you might be interested in sampling."

He held his spoon out to her. "Are you sure?"

He nodded. "Of course. Dig in."

She slipped his spoon into the creamy red soup dotted with pieces of fresh basil. It tasted fresh and was the perfect temperature. "Delicious," she said, returning his spoon.

As soon as they finished, a staff member came to collect their empty plates and refilled their water. No sooner had he left, Cheryl and a man with glasses on top of his head, wearing a black chef's jacket, stepped up to the table.

"Lydia, this is my husband Cyrus."

Lydia wasn't sure whether she should stand up or not, but she stayed seated and shook hands with him. Heath stood and retrieved two chairs from an empty table and positioned them at the edge of their table. "Oh, thank you, Heath," said Cheryl, sitting in the one closest to him.

Cyrus sat and smiled. "I've only got a few minutes, but Heath sang your praises and said you've worked in many restaurants and were looking for a position."

Lydia reached down by her handbag and handed him the file folder. "Here's my resume. I went to culinary school and have worked in several restaurants in Portland. My most recent position was chef for an upscale restaurant in Walla Walla. I also was a partner in a food truck business and have worked in all sorts of small family-owned places."

Cyrus flipped open the folder and pulled the glasses down to his eyes. He nodded as he read. "Very impressive." He closed the folder and added, "We're busiest on the weekends, and with the start of the summer season, we're looking for more help. How would you feel about coming in tomorrow and working in the kitchen, preparing a few things? If it's a good fit for both of us, we could start you this weekend. We'd need you Friday through Sunday for dinner service."

Lydia's heart was pounding in her chest. She was sure everyone could hear it hammering but concentrated on her breathing. "That sounds terrific. I can definitely be here tomorrow."

Cyrus clapped his hands on his thighs. "Wonderful, we'll see you at four if that works?"

"I'll be here."

He stood and returned his chair to the empty table. "I need to get back to the kitchen but look forward to chatting tomorrow." He strode back through the doorway, and Cheryl smiled at Lydia.

"I hope it works out, and you like it here. We about worked ourselves into the ground last summer. It would be wonderful to have someone capable in the kitchen, so we could take some time off."

With a relaxed smile, Lydia said, "I'm looking forward to learning more tomorrow, but I think it will be a great fit for me."

Cheryl left them with a promise that their entrees would be out in a few minutes and went to seat more guests. Heath raised his brows at Lydia. "Well, what do you think?"

"I've worked with husbands and wives in the past, and it's not always the best, but they seem nice, and I can imagine they need a break. It's hard work to do it all." She looked around the room. "I like the atmosphere, and the menu isn't overwhelming."

After a sip of water, she added, "Most of all, I need the job, so I'll make it work."

"I know they're obsessed with quality, which has earned them a real following in town. They shine during the summer when we have so many tourists in town for the festival and other activities. They cut back in the winter and are only open four days a week."

She sighed. "At least the worst part is over. I'm not worried about cooking for Cyrus, I just hate the whole interview and meeting part of a new job. I always feel like I'm fumbling and get tongue tied. I appreciate you doing the heavy lifting for me before we arrived."

He grinned. "No sweat. It's easy to rave about your food. I love to cook, but you are at another level." He chuckled as he reached for his glass. "You're also very lucky my trivia team is taking a break for the summer; otherwise, I would've made you join our team tonight at Rooster's. Usually, it's tacos and trivia for me on Tuesdays."

"I think you dodged a bullet. I wouldn't be good at trivia, unless it was food related."

The server arrived with their plates, and Lydia took a good look at the presentation, which was creative, with fresh rosemary on top of Heath's steak and fresh herbs on the mushroom risotto next to it. Her chicken smelled wonderful, and the creamy sauce with mushrooms was mouthwatering. Fresh herbs decorated the plate, and the garlic mashed potatoes were also sprinkled with fresh parsley.

Before she dug into her plate, Heath moved his closer to the center of the table. "You need to try this risotto. Spoiler alert—yours is better."

She laughed and took a forkful. It was good, but he was right. Hers was better. She tried a bite of her chicken, which was juicy and tender. She let the taste of the buttery chardonnay and the hint of lemon mingle in her mouth.

Heath cut into his steak. "If you're still up for the chili cookoff, I wanted to invite you over to the house on Thursday. We could cook together." He held up his hand. "I promise I won't cheat and will stick to my winning recipe. We have to have the entries down to the fairgrounds by five o'clock."

She grinned. "I don't want to be in your way."

"Trust me, our kitchen is big enough for two cooks. It'll be fun. Say yes."

She couldn't resist his smile or those blue eyes. "Yes."

CHAPTER NINE

T hursday morning, Lydia woke to a gentle rain shower. She threw on a robe with a hood and tucked Vera inside it before sprinting to the house. She came in through the mudroom to find everyone gathered around the island and a celebratory box of pastries from the Sugar Shack.

Her trial run at the Ranch House had gone well, and Cyrus and Cheryl hired her as a chef. Her first shift would be Friday, starting at three with the restaurant closing at nine. Last night, when she got home and shared the good news, they had gathered around her in a group hug, dancing around in a circle. The dogs looked at them as if they were crazy, but they soon couldn't resist getting in on the fun.

Harry had made an early morning run to the bakery and along with tea and coffee, Micki and Olivia poured sparkling apple juice into wine glasses. Lydia's heart warmed at the effort they put into the celebration. Meg grabbed two donuts, gave her mom a hug, and congratulated Lydia on her way out the door to the veterinary clinic.

As the three sisters waited on her, Lydia's heart filled with happiness. Nobody had made this much fuss over her since Jewel. While the pay was far lower than what she could get in a city, with her living at the farm, it would allow her to rebuild her savings. Along with her free meal during her work hours, Cyrus let Lydia know she was welcome to take leftovers home at the end of the night.

The restaurant had kitchen staff to help with the prep work early in the day, and Cyrus would work with her the first week to make sure she knew the ropes before even thinking of leaving her on her own. He also assured her, he and Cheryl could be there in minutes, as they lived only a few blocks away from the restaurant.

As the four of them nibbled on cinnamon rolls, donuts, and croissants, they chattered on about their excitement at Lydia's new job. Lydia reached for the paper she'd left on the counter with the various lavender treats she made over the last few days listed on it. Her eager samplers had rated each of them and given her comments.

"I see the lavender shortbread cookies, the iced lemon lavender cookies, lavender lemon bars, and the cupcakes with lavender buttercream are the favorites," said Lydia, smiling as she perused the list.

"Sadly, the lavender blackberry mini cheesecakes were my favorite," said Harry. "I know we can't offer anything that needs refrigeration, but those were the bomb."

The other two sisters nodded as they chewed. Olivia took a sip of tea and added, "I really liked that lavender lemonade you made. That would be popular, I think."

Micki pointed at the list. "Those iced cookies you decorated with the stencils are gorgeous. I think they're a must, and they taste wonderful." With an impish grin, she added, "I already took photos of them for the website."

Olivia cut off a chunk of her croissant. "Honestly,

everything you made was delicious. It might be fun to offer a variety, so visitors have to come back if we're out of their favorite one day."

Harry arched her brows. "Look at you. A marketing maven in our midst."

Lydia laughed. "I still want to make some lavender chocolate truffles and macarons, along with scones. I'll work on those this weekend."

Micki shook her head. "Don't rush. Just wait until your days off. We have plenty of time to load up photos and entice visitors."

Lydia shrugged. "I guess so. I feel bad since I intended to cook Sunday dinner for everyone each week, but with work, that won't be possible."

"I know Sunday dinner is traditional, but we could switch it up to Mondays." Harry glanced over at Olivia and Micki and raised her brows in a questioning look.

Micki nodded. "That works for me. It's also a great excuse to keep from going to Medford to see Jade on Mondays. With Meg off on Sundays, that's probably the day that's best for us to go on the weekends." The droop in her shoulders announced her lack of excitement at the prospect.

As they finished their breakfast treats, the three sisters offered Lydia the use of their vehicles, so Lydia wouldn't have to drive her motorhome and park it downtown. They didn't want her riding her bike at night. Lydia hated to borrow their cars, but protesting was a losing battle with the three of them. She finally relented and agreed to the plan.

Harry made sure she hadn't spilled any stray sugar on her blouse and gathered her handbag. "I'm off to work. My turn for dinner tonight. I'll pick up Rooster's unless you want pizza instead?"

They left it up to her, with Lydia reminding them they'd

have leftover chili for tomorrow. After giving Chief another pet, Harry went through the door with a wave. Lydia glanced at the time. "I best get a shower. I promised Heath I'd be there in an hour to make chili today."

Micki smiled. "Oh, that's right. What did you think of that kitchen?"

Lydia's eyes widened. "It's incredible. I'm sort of excited to cook in it. I knew from what you all said, the house was something, but when he pulled up to it Tuesday night after we had dinner, I think my jaw dropped to the ground. The whole place is like something out of a magazine. It reminded me of some fancy homes I've catered things at in Portland."

Olivia collected the plates and rinsed them. "Heath's a great cook and really seems to enjoy it. I'm sure you'll have a fun day."

Lydia finished the last of her sparkling juice. "We have to have the chili entries at the fairgrounds by five o'clock, so the judges can taste them. I want to get an early start, since I think the flavors are enriched when the chili cooks slowly for several hours."

"I'm home all day working or in the garden, so feel free to take my car," said Micki.

Lydia took her glass to the sink. "I can ride my bike. The exercise will do me good, and Heath can bring me home."

"It's up to you, but it's there if you need it," said Micki. "Speaking of work, I need to get on it. Best of luck on the chili contest."

Olivia shut the dishwasher and wiped her hands on a towel. "I'm going to take the dogs for a walk this morning. Vera can hang with us."

Lydia looked over at her tiny girl, snuggled in with the goldens. "She's adapting quite well to having siblings."

"I think we all are," said Olivia, with a shy smile.

Lydia gave Vera a quick pet on the head and then made sure to do the same for the other three dogs before hurrying to the master bathroom for a shower.

Once she was ready, she said goodbye to Micki and with the rain, opted to take her up on her offer of using her car. Heath gave her the code to their gate Tuesday night, but she didn't need to use it. The gate was open, and she drove through it.

The property was even more impressive in daylight. She wound her way down the long driveway, bordered by green pastures and white fences, and parked under the portico, where a huge bronze statue of a horse made her gasp. Tuesday night, Heath had parked in the back, and she never saw the horse.

She couldn't stop staring at it. Heath opened the front door and snapped her out of her trance. "Morning," he said with a slow smile. "Come on in."

"Sorry, that horse captured my attention. It's so lifelike." She grabbed her bag with the two ingredients she wanted to make sure she used and followed him inside.

He led her to the huge kitchen, where he had two large pots set up on opposite ends of the cooktop. There was plenty of counterspace on each side of the cooktop to allow for each of them to work. Jars of spices, onions, garlic, peppers, wine, broth, tomato sauce and paste, along with crushed and diced tomatoes, several types of beans, and bottles of beer were lined up on the counter.

"I've got the ground chuck and sirloin in the fridge, and I like to add a bit of diced chuck steak, so that's available if you want any. Oh, and the bacon you requested." Heath put an apron over his head and tied the strings around his waist. He handed her another one from the hook on the wall.

She slipped it on and stepped toward the cooktop. "Which side is mine?"

He pointed and said, "I'm used to working on the left, so you can have the right side.

"Works for me," she said, taking her cocoa powder and maple syrup out of her tote bag.

He eyed the new ingredients she added to the countertop. "Secret ingredients?" He raised his brows. "I won't breathe a word. I use beer in mine, and I think that's what makes it so good."

He stepped to the fridge and retrieved the meat and bacon.

She took a glass bowl and measured out portions of chili powder, paprika, cumin, salt, pepper, and cayenne to make her seasoning. She started with bacon, chopping it and adding it to the pan to crisp. He added oil to his pan and the pieces of chuck steak. She noticed a stained and well-worn recipe card on his part of the counter. "Are you using a family recipe?"

He moved his head from side to side as he stirred the meat. "Sort of. I started with my mom's basic recipe and over the years, added a few things and enhanced it."

She minced the garlic and diced the yellow onions and an orange pepper while she waited for the bacon to cook. The rich aroma of it and that of the steak sizzling in Heath's pot filled the air. "Where are your dogs hiding?"

Heath chuckled. "Maverick and Ace went with Clay. He's checking on some cows and fences, then running some errands. They'd just be watching us and drooling all over the floor if they were in here."

He removed his steak and added in the ground beef

mixture before dicing the onions. She removed the bacon to let it drain on a paper towel, drained off most of the grease, and added in the ground beef mixture. She stirred it and broke it up, letting it partially cook before removing it and scraping the onion and pepper from her cutting board into the pan. After letting them cook for a few minutes, she added in the garlic, stirred it, and breathed in the incredible fragrance. She added the beef back into the pan, mixing it in well, and then sprinkled in her spice mixture.

After stirring it together, she added in cocoa powder. Next came tomato puree, sauce, and both crushed and diced tomatoes. She didn't measure anything, just went by sight and texture to get the right portions. After adding in the cooked bacon, she stirred it together and let it cook for a few minutes before using a spoon to taste it.

She added in some maple syrup and stirred it again, letting it cook while she cleaned up some of her mess. She came back to it and gave it another taste, adding a bit more syrup.

With her dishes done, she wandered back to the pot and checked on the chili. It was simmering nicely. She glanced over at Heath's, which also looked delicious. He was opening a bottle of beer and smiling at her. "You're all done?"

The doorbell interrupted them. He wiped his hands on a towel. "I'll be right back. Can you keep an eye on that?"

"Sure, take your time."

He hurried down the hallway. She gave the chili a stir and added in the beer he had been about to pour. She glanced over at his recipe card. She smiled at his notes next to his mother's script.

She couldn't resist tasting his chili and dipped a spoon into the pot. She nodded as she tasted. It was good. Better than good. She rinsed the spoon and retrieved a pitcher of iced tea from the fridge. She poured them each a glass and sat at the island counter to wait for her chili to finish cooking.

After a few minutes, he poked his head around the corner. His jovial smile was gone, and his face was pale. "I'll be a few more minutes." He glanced at the cooktop, worry etched on his face.

"Don't worry. I added the beer and will keep my eye on it. I can finish it off, so don't rush."

He nodded and disappeared without a word.

Staring at the archway where he'd been, she frowned. Something was definitely wrong. She hoped it wasn't bad news.

She finished her tea, tasted her chili again, and added in two kinds of beans, stirring it together and lowering the heat.

After checking the recipe again, she did the same for Heath's pot, using both pinto and kidney beans, and then cleaned up his dishes and countertop. With it being past lunchtime, she searched the fridge and put together a mini charcuterie board filled with fruit, veggies, cheese, and some salami.

As she searched the pantry for some crackers, Heath returned to the kitchen. The color hadn't returned to his cheeks, and his easy smile was nowhere to be found. Instead of sparkling, his blue eyes were filled with anguish.

He went straight to his pot of chili, took a bite, and stirred it. He turned toward her. "Thanks for finishing it up. Sorry I was gone so long."

Her forehead creased with concern. "Are you okay?"

He leaned against the counter and shook his head. "I honestly don't know. I think I might have a daughter."

CHAPTER TEN

H is words made Lydia drop the crackers she was arranging. "What?"

"Exactly," he said. He moved to a chair at the island counter and took a long swallow from the watered-down glass of iced tea. "I have no idea what to make of it all."

She brought the snacks with her, along with the pitcher of tea, and took a seat next to him. "Have something to eat and tell me what happened."

He shook his head. "I don't think I can eat anything. This is unbelievable." He drummed his fingers on the granite. "Cassidy Bennet, that's the young woman who came to see me. Her mother died recently. Her name was Amy Godwin. She grew up in Medford. I remember her from the rodeo circuit. The last time I saw her, I was a senior in high school, seventeen years old."

He took another drink from his glass and popped two grapes into his mouth. She didn't press him or hurry him. He struggled to get the words out. "Geez, this is not good. Amy was a few years older than me. Anyway, at the end of the year, a few weeks before graduation, I was at a rodeo event in Medford, and she was there. She was gorgeous. We were out with a group of people and drinking beer. Both of us tipsy and stupid. One thing led to another. We ending up sleeping together."

He hung his head. "For the first time, I'm glad my parents are gone. I don't think I could handle telling them this." Tears glinted in his eyes.

She reached for his hand. "Teenagers do dumb things. Don't be so hard on yourself."

"My ego was stoked having an older girl interested in me. I remember being head over heels for her. I asked if I could call her. That's when she giggled and told me no, that wasn't a good idea. She was getting married the next weekend."

Lydia winced for him. Embarrassment colored his cheeks, and his shoulders drooped even more. "Oh, no."

After a bite of cheese, he continued, "I was shocked but moved on quickly. I had things to do to get ready for college and never gave Amy another thought." He sighed. "Until today."

"How did she find you?"

"Her dad died in an accident a few years ago, and then Amy got cancer. She passed away about a month ago and before she died, she told Amy that her dad wasn't her biological dad. She gave her my name and told her the story."

Lydia's eyes widened. "I take it you believe her?"

With a slow nod, he met her eyes. "Yeah. Cassidy seems like a sweet girl. Woman, gosh, she's thirty years old. Dark hair, like Amy. Blue eyes, like mine."

"Where does she live?"

"About six hours away. In the Bay Area. She's in advertising. She's staying at the Lavender Valley Inn." He stood and paced around the kitchen. "I don't know what to do. I feel like I should offer to let her stay here, but I need to figure things out."

"What's your impression of her? Does she seem sincere?"

He wandered to the French doors and opened them. "Are you hot in here? It seems really warm." He stepped outside and stood at the railing, overlooking the pond.

She carried both of their iced teas to the table and set them down, then fetched the snacks and some napkins. After placing them on the table, she joined him at the railing, resting her arm against his.

He kept staring at the pond. "She's distraught about losing her mom. She's upset with her for not telling her the truth. She's confused. I believe her when she says she wants to get to know me. She has no brothers or sisters and is looking for her family. I guess that's me."

"If you want to verify her information, I bet Buck or Harry could help."

He shrugged. "She left me a folder full of all her pertinent information. Birth certificate, driver's license, all her contact information. College records, employment history. She said she'd do a DNA test. She included photos of her with Amy and her dad Ryan. Even a letter to me from Amy." He sighed. "I'll have Buck take a look, for sure, but I don't think she's making it up."

"Wow. What did the letter say?"

He shook his head. "I don't know. I'm not brave enough to read it right now."

Lydia coaxed him to eat a few bites and kept her eye on both of their pots of chili. She sat with him on the patio, listening as he rambled on about the situation with Amy and sitting quietly as he stared at the pond.

As the hours ticked by, she tapped him on the shoulder. "How about I package up the chili, and I'll drop it off at the fairgrounds. Just tell me where to go."

"You don't need to worry about mine. The chili contest is the least of my worries."

"I'll take them both, just point me in the right direction."

He explained the containers were on the counter by the fridge, along with the labels. "The judging takes place in the main room off the kitchen. You can't miss it."

She went inside and found the heavy foil containers and the entry forms with the tear off labels printed only with the number of the contestant. She went about filling her container first and attached her number to the container and the lid and then washed the ladle and did the same for his.

The containers were hot, and she carefully put them in a box Heath had prepared and turned off the cooktop. As she was getting ready to leave, Clay and the two dogs came through the archway. The furry friends dashed through to the patio where Heath was still sitting.

"How's the chili cookoff going?" Clay smiled at her and wandered to the cooktop to take a look.

"Chili's fine." She pointed outside. "Heath's had a bit of a surprise."

The wrinkle in his forehead deepened. "That doesn't sound good."

"I'll let him tell you. He's upset, so be gentle with him. I'm going to take off and drop these off for the judges." She eyed the pots on the stove. "I'll come back and take care of the leftovers."

Clay glanced toward the patio, where Heath sat, ignoring the dogs. Worry filled his eyes. "He doesn't look good at all.

That's so unlike him. Of the two of us, he's always happy and looking at the positive. Now, I'm more than worried."

Lydia grimaced. "It's not my place to say anything. He's just had some news, and it's upset him. My best advice is not to pressure him and give him some time to tell you."

She wandered out to the patio. Heath was sitting at the table, his head in his hands. She tapped him on the shoulder. "I'm off to take these to the fairgrounds. I'll be back soon and take care of the rest of the chili."

He lifted his head and met her eyes. "Thanks, Lydia. I'm sorry today was a fiasco."

She shook her head and smiled. "Don't apologize. You've got a lot to deal with. I'll see you soon."

He started to slide his chair out, and she put a hand on his back. "No, don't get up. I can see myself out."

He nodded, and Clay came through the door as she was stepping back inside the house. He glanced over at her and lowered his voice. "Hurry back. I might need your help. Don't bother with the doorbell or knocking, just come on in."

She nodded, collected the chili, and hurried to Micki's SUV. The fairgrounds were about five miles on the other side of town, but she had plenty of time. Her thoughts drifted to Heath on the drive. She hated seeing him so distraught and couldn't imagine how he was feeling.

Heath's directions were spot-on, and she checked in at the registration table. She submitted Heath's first and then as she started to sign her name on the clipboard, decided not to enter her chili. She toted it back to the car and smiled. Heath needed the boost of a win now more than ever.

She popped by the farm on the way home and dropped off her entry container. She didn't want to risk Heath seeing it.

Harry was pulling in as Lydia climbed the porch steps. She held bags of takeout from Rooster's. Lydia held the door for her, and she stepped through it and settled the bags on the dining room table. "Dinner is served," she said with a chuckle.

Then, she glanced at the foil pan in Lydia's hands. "Is that your chili entry?"

"Yeah," she said, with a shrug. She lowered her voice. "It's a long story, but I decided not to enter it. I don't want Heath or Clay to know, though, so just keep it between us." She found a glass bowl with a lid and transferred the chili into it and popped it in the fridge.

Harry tilted her head. "Okay. I won't ask."

"I'll tell you later. I'm going to run back over to Heath's and clean up the chili. He's had a bit of a rotten day." She glanced at the takeout burgers. "Just save me a burger or if anyone wants more, feel free to eat it. I shouldn't be too long. I'll leave Micki's car here in case she needs it."

She dashed out before Micki or Olivia saw her, hopped on her bicycle, and rode the short distance down the road. As she meandered down the long driveway, she suspected it would have been quicker to go through the field and use the gate between the two properties.

It felt good to exercise her legs, but she was certain they'd be sore tomorrow. She parked in front, gawking at the bronze horse for a few moments before opening the door. She was quiet but couldn't hide from the two dogs, who greeted her in the kitchen.

Clay and Heath were outside on the patio, huddled close together. She noticed Clay's hand on his brother's shoulder.

She used the ladle and scooped out Heath's chili into one

of the containers he'd left on the counter. She left some in the pot and turned the heat on low to keep it warm, in case they opted to eat it for dinner. She found a bowl in the cupboard and put a scoop of her chili in it. In her rush to get things packed up for the contest, she forgot to taste the finished product.

A smile filled her face as she finished off the bite. It was perfect. Over the years, she'd tried various ingredients like brown sugar, honey, and white sugar to cut the acidity of the tomatoes, but maple syrup was her favorite secret. It, with the bacon, really set off the flavors in the rich dish.

With her pot empty, she set it in the sink and filled it with water. With the chores done, she risked a glimpse outside. Heath and Clay were deep in conversation, and the last thing she wanted to do was interrupt them. As she contemplated leaving, she thought of something else she could do.

Cookies. They made everything better. At least she liked to think so. Earlier, she glimpsed everything she could need in the pantry. She gathered the ingredients and whisked together the bread flour, her secret to a thick fluffy cookie, baking powder, baking soda, and salt. Then she used the stand mixer on the counter to soften the butter and mix in the sugars.

While it mixed, she retrieved baking sheets from the cabinet and lined them with parchment paper. She added the dry ingredients to the mixer and as soon as they came together, shut it off. Then, by hand, she mixed in chocolate chips and pecans. The dough was thick and heavy, and it took some effort to incorporate it.

After dropping scoops of dough onto the prepared sheets, she slipped them into the freezer. That was another secret to her fabulous cookies. Once the sheets were in the freezer, she cleaned up her mess and retrieved three bottles of beer from the fridge.

After catching Clay's eye and getting a nod, she stepped onto the patio. She placed the bottles on the table, noticing a thick file folder and an envelope bearing Heath's name. She glanced down at Heath. "I thought it might be a good time for a beer."

His lips turned up a bit, and he reached out for one, handing the other to Clay. "Thanks, Lydia. A keg might be a better idea." He took a long swallow and leaned back in his chair.

She pointed back at the kitchen. "I left some of your chili warming if you're hungry."

Clay nodded. "I could eat. Anybody else?"

Lydia smiled. "I'd love some. I confess I had a tiny taste, and it was so yummy. I'd love a bowl. Can I help?"

Clay shook his head. "Just relax. I've got it."

Heath took another sip and met Lydia's eyes. "Clay called Buck, and he's going to verify Cassidy's information. He's got access to a database and thought he could get most of it done tonight. He'll call as soon as he has news."

She nodded. "That's good. Smart. With all the crazy stuff going on in the world, it makes sense to check things."

"If she's my daughter, and at this point, I think she is, there's not much I can do except get to know her and try to have some sort of relationship."

"How long is she in Lavender Valley?"

"She's just here for the Memorial Day weekend. She has a flight back on Monday. Clay thought if she checks out, we ought to have her stay here at the ranch. We've got plenty of guest rooms."

"I think that would be nice. I can relate to searching for a family. My life was pretty much chaos until I came to live with Jewel and Chuck. We were like a real family. I'm sure Cassidy is heartbroken with the recent loss of her mother. This has to be hard for her."

Heath sighed. "My head has been spinning since she came, and I've been worrying more about me and how this will impact me. What people will think. I mean what kind of a guy finds out he's got a kid when he's almost fifty years old?"

"That wasn't your choice though, Heath. It's not like you abandoned her or rejected her. You made a mistake when you were seventeen. I honestly don't think anyone will judge you. I think Cassidy needs you, now more than ever."

He shook his head. "I'm so mad at myself. I felt duped back then when Amy said she was getting married. Like she used me, but I consoled myself with the fact she was hot and older. It's different for guys, I know."

Lydia leaned back and laughed. "The understatement of the century."

Clay came through the door carrying a tray. He set it on the table, passed out bowls of chili, and added a bowl of shredded cheese to the table. He handed each of them a tall glass of iced tea and caught Lydia's eye. "By the way, I saw some trays of cookies in the freezer. Is that you're doing?"

"Cookies always help me feel better, so I made my famous chocolate chip and pecan recipe. I freeze them before I bake them. I'll pop them in when we're done eating, and you can have them for dessert."

Heath reached for the cheese. "Now you sound like our mom. She thought cookies were also the answer to our problems." He smiled at her. "Not that I disagree, and that was kind of you."

After Clay took a seat, he smiled at Lydia. "I found your chili in the fridge and put some on the stove to warm. I'm dying to taste yours. I'll have to see if I think it's worthy of dethroning this big guy." He grinned at his brother before glancing at Lydia.

A hint of the usual sparkle returned to Heath's eyes, along with a grin. "Hers is over the top. I got a look at her secret ingredients, and I snuck a taste when she wasn't looking. I suspect we'll have a new winner tomorrow."

Clay chuckled. "It's good to prepare yourself."

Lydia hid her smile behind a heaping spoonful of Heath's chili.

CHAPTER ELEVEN

Curled next to Vera, Lydia slept in on Friday morning. With it being her first shift at the Ranch House and staying up later than she expected last night, she reasoned she needed the extra sleep.

Last night, after their chili dinner, Lydia baked cookies while Clay did the dishes. Heath continued to sit on the patio with the dogs by his side, coming to grips with the idea of being a father to a grown woman. While they were eating cookies, Buck called and let Heath know he was able to verify everything Cassidy told him. He stressed his research was all done online and using databases, so he hadn't personally talked to her boss, coworkers, or neighbors, but felt confident she was being truthful.

With that news, Heath relaxed more, and he and Clay put together a plan to invite Cassidy to stay at the ranch over the weekend. They mentioned hosting a brunch on Sunday, and Lydia offered to help cook.

It was dark when she was ready to ride home, and Clay insisted on giving her a ride. Neither of the brothers would budge, even though Heath had consumed too many beers to drive. She relented and let Clay put her bike in the back of his truck.

It proved to be a good idea, since Harry was still awake, minding Vera. The others had turned in for the evening. After thanking Harry for waiting up, Lydia collected Vera and made her way to the motorhome, leaving Clay and Harry on the porch.

The purr of his truck starting an hour later filtered through Lydia's foggy early sleep and made her smile. She was certain he had explained Heath's news to her. By Sunday, they'd all know the story, since Heath planned to introduce Cassidy to everyone at brunch.

By the time Lydia and Vera found their way to the house, Harry was gone, Olivia was getting ready for a trip to pick up another rescue and Micki was in the cottage working on her lavender products.

While Vera ate her breakfast, Lydia took a shower. Using the lavender scrubs left her skin so smooth and hydrated. It was rare that she indulged in anything beyond the basics when it came to beauty and self-care, but testing the samples made her a believer.

She slathered on more of the lavender body butter and let it soak in while she finished getting ready. She slipped on jeans and a soft T-shirt, left her hair to dry naturally, and gulped down a piece of toast and a cup of coffee while she visited with Vera in the kitchen.

She promised Micki she'd help her with the labeling and packaging today before she left for her shift at the restaurant. She finished her coffee, rinsed the cup, and hurried Vera outside.

She found Micki seated at the long table running across the living area. She looked up from the bottle she was labeling. "Morning," she said, patting the chair next to hers. "Come on over, and I'll show you what to do."

Lydia was in charge of attaching the ingredient labels, and Micki affixed the logo and price. As they worked, they chatted. "Are you excited about your new job?" asked Micki.

"Yeah, excited and a bit anxious. It's always an adjustment to gel with the existing staff. It's small though, so I suspect it won't be hard."

"It's a great restaurant. Their food is delish. The Back Door Bistro is also excellent. Their panzanella is the best I've ever eaten."

"Oh, that's a great dish. We'll have to make it one night. Especially, when your garden starts to produce."

Micki moved a full box of product from their assembly line to the shelves. "I'm getting more and more excited for the festival. I've been chatting with the artist about the paint and sip event. She mocked up some paintings, and they're perfect. Sunflowers, lavender, and dahlias."

"Oh, that will be great. Those are always popular events."

"I added photos of your cookies to the website this morning. I was hoping you could make some for the paint and sip events, too."

"Sure, I'd be happy to. I'm going to test out scones this weekend. Did Harry tell you Clay and Heath invited everyone to brunch on Sunday? I offered to help and thought I'd make scones and try them out on everyone."

Micki nodded as she worked on a label. "Yes, she mentioned that. Meg and I are going to run to Medford to see Jade Sunday." She rolled her eyes and sighed. "We'll do brunch first, though. Spending time with her is not my favorite activity."

"Is she getting better?"

With a shrug, Micki reached for another label. "I think

physically things are healing, but so far, her memory hasn't returned." She shook her head. "That makes me mad sometimes, since I can remember every horrible thing she and my mother did to me. Jade can just sit there in oblivion. She's quiet, which is also unusual. She's got a big mouth and normally, it's always in motion."

"I'm sorry you're stuck in this situation." Lydia slid another bottle down the table.

Micki smiled. "All I know is being here with my sisters of the heart makes it much easier to deal with this latest pothole on my path. Also, having my daughter back in my life is a true blessing. Whenever I get bogged down with my feelings toward Jade, I remind myself where I was a few months ago. With all of you and Meg and now Buck, I can weather any storm."

Lydia let her words sink in and breathed in the lovely scent of the products they were labeling. "Being here, like you say, is comforting. When I came here more than thirty years ago, it was the first time I felt loved and part of a real family. Since then, I've been on my own and until now, I don't think I realized what I was missing. It's so nice not to feel alone."

Micki slipped her arm around Lydia. "You'll never have to be alone again. We'll all be here for you no matter what. That's what families do."

Lydia checked the mirror one more time. Her hair was in the signature messy updo she'd perfected over the years of working in the industry. The uniforms she brought home from the restaurant fit, and she ran her hand down the striped, black pants. They were comfortable, and the short black sleeve chef's jacket looked crisp and professional. It also had a couple of mesh panels along the side that would keep her cool.

She added the black cap that was tied in the back over her hair. She smiled as she tied it, remembering the tall white chef's hat she had to wear in culinary school. It was so not her style, and she was glad the industry had evolved into something less obnoxious.

She slipped into the expensive clogs she always wore when working. They were black with a metallic rose print on them. Long ago, one of her instructors at culinary school gave her advice. Never skimp on shoes or knives, and Lydia took it to heart. She removed her knife roll from the drawer in the motorhome.

Vera was sitting on the couch, watching her as she gathered her things. "Come on, Vera," she said. "You're going to stay with the others while I'm at work."

The little dog hurried out the door and bounced down the steps. Olivia and Micki were in the kitchen and gave her a wolf whistle when she walked through the door. She grinned at them and bowed.

"You look very professional," said Olivia. She handed Lydia the keys to her SUV.

Lydia slipped the keys into her pocket. "Thank you. Are you sure you won't need your car?"

Olivia picked up Vera and cuddled her in her arms. "Positive. We're all staying home tonight and having your chili for dinner."

Micki finished pouring her iced tea. "We'll have plenty of cars available if anyone needs to go to town."

"Okay, I'll see you all when I get home. Wish me luck." She took hold of her leather knife roll and her handbag and went through the door.

She parked in the employee lot around the back of the house and went through the service entrance. Cheryl and Cyrus were in the kitchen, along with Angus, the young sous chef she met when she auditioned.

She said hello and stashed her handbag in the small employee lounge and picked up an apron she tied around her waist. She washed her hands at the sink and joined the others.

The kitchen, unlike the rest of the house, was sleek and modern. It was set up with a large center island and workspace along the perimeter. There were two doors, one where only the dirty dishes came through to the dishwashing area and the other where servers collected the plates to deliver to customers.

Stainless steel dominated every surface, and it was all spotless and clean. Angus was busy chopping vegetables, and the aroma of fresh baked bread hung in the air. Cyrus was putting the finishing touches on the soup, a potato leek.

He smiled as she looked over the edge of the pot. "We've got a special rib eye, honey garlic salmon, and I thought you might make that pasta you talked about. It's a great dish for the weather we're having." He pointed at the chef's workspace at the island.

"Sounds great," Lydia said, taking her worn leather knife roll and settling in at the island.

She gathered lemons, capers, white wine, garlic, basil, and tomatoes. Cyrus also asked her to make the panzanella salad. She went about her tasks, lost in the familiar world, where she could create the food she loved. The colorful veggies and wonderful scents of garlic and basil made her heart sing.

Soon, the kitchen helpers arrived, and Cyrus introduced her while Cheryl made sure the front of the house was ready for their guests. The kitchen was a hive of activity and by the time the servers and wait staff arrived, all the preparation was done, and they were ready.

Lydia's pasta dish was a huge hit with the diners, and salmon and rib eyes were flying out of the kitchen as quick as they could make them. Things were slowing down around eight o'clock when Cheryl came into the kitchen.

"Lydia, could you spare a few minutes? A table requested to see you."

She nodded and wiped her hands before following Cheryl to the dining area. She led her to the quiet room where she and Heath had eaten earlier in the week. With a wave of her hand, Cheryl presented the table.

When she saw Heath, Clay, and a young woman with dark hair and stunning blue eyes that matched Heath's, relief flooded over her, and Lydia grinned.

Heath stood and met Lydia's eyes. "We just had a delicious meal, and I was telling Cassidy about you being a chef."

He put his hand on the young woman's shoulders. "Lydia, this is my daughter Cassidy. She's staying at the ranch with us this weekend."

Lydia extended her hand. "It's wonderful to meet you. I'm glad you enjoyed your meal."

Cassidy shook her hand and then gestured to her empty bowl that had held Lydia's pasta. "This was so delicious."

"It's a nice light dish for summer." Lydia looked at Clay's plate and then Heath's. "I bet you boys had the rib eyes, right?"

Heath grinned. "And the mushroom risotto."

The brothers chuckled. Clay pointed at his empty plate. "Top notch, as always. Oh, and by the way, Heath got word today; he's retained his title as the Chili King."

"Wow, congratulations," said Lydia, glancing over at him. "Yours is excellent, so I'm not surprised."

Heath frowned. "I'm more than a little surprised. I actually thought yours was better, and you didn't even place in the top three."

She shrugged. "Well, judging is always subjective. They probably know what they like, and mine might have been too different for them."

Lydia glanced behind her. "I better get back to the kitchen. I don't want to mess up on my first night. I'm glad you enjoyed the food, and I'll see you on Sunday for brunch. It was great to meet you, Cassidy."

"You, too. Heath told me you're helping cook on Sunday, so I'm looking forward to that." She had a sweet smile and a softness about her.

As she started to walk away, Heath cleared his throat. "Oh, Lydia, I thought we might stop by and show Cassidy the lavender farm tomorrow."

"Sure, I'll be around. I start work at three, but I'll be home until then, and Micki should be there. Feel free to stop by." She waved and hurried to the kitchen.

As she made the turn toward the door, a hand gripped her arm. She turned and saw Clay. "Hey, sorry to startle you. I just wanted to thank you."

She frowned. "For what?"

"I have a friend who helps with the rodeo and the chili cookoff. I told him I couldn't believe your chili didn't place. He said you didn't have an entry. That's when I figured it out."

She smiled but didn't say anything.

"I appreciate you being so kind to Heath. He was struggling and when he got the news he won, it really boosted his mood."

She lowered her voice. "Promise me he'll never find out."

He shook his head. "He won't. It was kind of you to do that for him."

She winked and said, "He might not be so lucky next time."

CHAPTER TWELVE

Sunday morning dawned with a gorgeous blue sky and sunshine. Lydia hurried to get dressed, rousted Vera off her bed, and found Olivia in the kitchen, getting bowls ready for the dogs. "Morning, Lydia. Vera is just in time for breakfast."

"Aww, thanks for taking care of her. I think she's adapting to being part of a pack instead of just the two of us."

"Yes, the goldens watch over her, and Hope, especially, is always by her side." She put the bowls on the floor, and the dogs waited for her to give the okay for them to eat.

Lydia poured a cup of coffee and took a few sips. "I'm going to head over to Heath's to help get brunch prepped."

"Clay said to bring the dogs when we come, so I'll just bring Vera with the rest of the gang. I think he said to be there around ten."

Lydia swallowed the rest of her coffee. "I need to get going. See you when you get there." She hurried to her bicycle and opted to try the pathway through the field. Even stopping to open and close the gate, it was quicker than taking the highway and the long driveway that led to the Nolan house.

She parked and as Heath instructed, let herself in through the front door. She found Heath in the kitchen, the dogs sitting and watching his every move. They noticed her long before he did and rushed to greet her.

He turned from dicing fruit and smiled at her. "Morning, Lydia. Thanks again for helping."

She washed her hands and donned an apron. "This will be fun. I've been dying to ask how it's going with Cassidy. She looked very happy at dinner the other night."

He smiled. "It's all good, I think. After the initial shock wore off a bit and with Clay's help, I snapped out of it, I guess. She's a sweet young woman and like you said, she's just looking for her family. I can't deny her that and while I wish Amy would have told me long before now, I can't change the past."

"She's a lucky gal. You and Clay are a wonderful family." As she talked, she gathered the ingredients for quiche and put together the pie crusts. Once the crusts were in the oven to prebake, she diced the bacon and started it cooking.

"Cassidy is great. She's smart and funny, and it's been nice to have her here. I think she's nervous about meeting everyone today." Heath layered strips of bacon on baking sheets covered with parchment paper.

"She's gorgeous and seemed very nice at dinner. I'm glad things worked out for both of you." She whisked the eggs, grated the cheese, and finished adding the filling to the crusts and moved to making scones.

Heath was busy mixing together butter and brown sugar for the topping on his baked french toast casserole. "I know my parents would be disappointed in me and how this all came about, but part of me is really sad they aren't here to meet their granddaughter. I know they would have loved her. Mom would be over the moon to have a girl in the family. Clay and I took her on a horseback ride yesterday. Her first time on a horse."

"Oh, I bet she loved it. Hopefully, Cassidy will be able to come back and visit. This property is such a one-of-a-kind place. I bet she'll feel more connected if she spends some time here, learning the history."

He nodded. "Yeah, I think so, too. She lives in an apartment and sounds like she works a ton of hours, so I think being here would be a true vacation for her. I've made it clear she's welcome, and I'm sure she'll be back. I hinted at the Lavender Festival."

"Oh, yeah, that would be a fun time for her to be here." She finished off the blueberry scone dough and moved on to the lemon with lavender she wanted to try.

He watched as she grated frozen butter. "That's interesting."

She smiled and explained the secret to flaky scones was not to overwork the dough and to keep the butter cold. "I'll put these in the fridge before I bake them to make sure they don't overspread when they bake."

He leaned back against the counter and smiled. "You're really a joy to watch in the kitchen. It's clear you're doing what you love when you're cooking. You sort of have this glow about you."

She blushed, her cheeks beyond rosy. "Okay, you're embarrassing me now." She finished shaping the lemon and lavender dough and cut it into wedges. She popped both sheets into the fridge.

"This kitchen is a true masterpiece. I love all the

workspace and the huge built-in fridge and freezer space. It's better than some commercial kitchens."

He glanced around the space and nodded. "Mom had excellent taste."

Cassidy came through the archway, smiling. "Something smells yummy."

Heath grinned at her. "Morning, Cassidy. Lydia and I have been slaving away on brunch." He moved to the coffee maker and poured a cup for her. "Here you go."

She took the cup and doctored it with cream and sugar. "What can I do to help? I'm almost useless in the kitchen, but I can set the table or do dishes."

Heath glanced out at the patio. "I thought we could eat outside. It's a beautiful morning. We can set up the food in here, buffet style. Cassidy, I'll show you where things are, and you can work on setting the table. We have twelve coming this morning."

Heath drained the bacon and placed it on a platter in the warming oven. He checked on his french toast casserole and the quiches, while Lydia placed the sheets of scones into the now vacant second oven.

She made the icing for them while they baked. While she was doing that, the doorbell rang, and Clay led the guests to the kitchen. Along with all her sisters of the heart, Meg and Buck came through the archway. Olivia, carrying Vera, herded the dogs outside where they could play together in a fenced area near the patio. Lydia wiped her hands and after saying hello to everyone, went out to check on Vera.

She was romping in the grass with the others, happy as she could be. Lydia stood next to Olivia for a few minutes and then wandered back to the main patio. Clay and Cassidy set up a beverage table next to the grill and enticed everyone out of the kitchen. Lydia poured herself an iced tea and added a splash of lemonade. She drank it down in two gulps.

She left her glass at a place setting on the table and hurried inside to check on the scones. They needed a few more minutes. As she was checking the quiches, Duke and May arrived and with them, an older gentleman he introduced as his father Leland. Next to Leland was a gorgeous golden retriever named Leo. Duke explained Leo and Hope were siblings. Lydia petted the top of his head and extended her hand to Leland. He shook it in both of his. "Wonderful to meet you, Lydia. Duke and Olivia say we're in for a real treat having you preparing brunch today."

"Well, I'm just helping Heath, but I do hope you'll try the lavender scones. I'm working on perfecting them for the festival."

His eyes sparkled. "Oh, that sounds good. I'll be sure to have one." Duke led them through and out to the patio.

She overheard May tell everyone her husband got called in to work at the last minute, so he wouldn't be able to join them.

Heath caught Lydia's eye. "He's a great man and a wonderful veterinarian. Duke worked with him until last year. Leland drops in to visit, but he's retired. Leo watches over him and with May's recent injuries, Olivia has been pitching in to help. They're a wonderful family."

"I could tell that the moment I met May in her store. You've all got something really special here." She turned her attention to the oven. The quiches were done, and she pulled them out and set them on a rack.

By then, the scones were done, and she took them from the oven, let them cool for a few minutes, and drizzled the lemon and lavender icing over them. They looked delicious with the coarse sugar on top and the specs of lavender throughout. The traditional blueberry ones smelled delicious and were bursting with the colorful berries. She used the vanilla icing on them and added both flavors to the serving platter.

While she sliced the warm quiche, Heath pulled his french toast casserole from the oven and plated up the bacon. The intoxicating aroma of brown sugar and bacon filled the air. After adding the fruit salad to the buffet, they both looked at each other and nodded.

"I think we've got it all ready," said Lydia, glancing around to make sure they hadn't forgotten anything.

Heath stepped onto the patio and hollered, "Come and get it."

As she watched the guests load their plates and comment on the delicious food, she recalled Heath's comments about her love for creating in the kitchen. He was right, of course. She always got a thrill when someone bit into something she made, and their eyes widened while they chewed and smiled. She didn't do it for the praise from others, but there was no denying the boost their kind comments provided.

Over her career, she'd suffered plenty of failures and missed the mark on some ideas, but she always learned from her mistakes and when working with new chefs or cooks, learned a few tricks and incorporated them in her cooking.

She and Heath were the last to fill their plates. He grinned as he added a huge square of his casserole, dripping in caramelized sugar and loaded with pecans, to his plate. He selected a piece of quiche and a blueberry scone. "I couldn't have done all this without your help, plus these look so good."

"I'm anxious to try the lavender ones. I've been working on some special treats for the festival and incorporating lavender."

She took her plate and found her seat next to Heath, who was at the head of the table and across from Cassidy.

Everyone was gathered around the table waiting for them before they dug into their plates. Heath set his plate down and remained standing. He took his glass of orange juice and raised it. "Thank you all for coming and giving me the opportunity to welcome Cassidy to the family. She's leaving tomorrow, but I'm trying to talk her into coming back for the festival, so maybe you can help me out and twist her arm today."

Everyone laughed and smiled at the young woman, whose cheeks were getting pinker by the second.

"Seriously though, I'm so thankful for this opportunity to spend time with her and show her around the ranch and Lavender Valley." He glanced over at Cassidy. "Thank you, Cassidy, for being brave and coming here. I know it wasn't easy but know you're part of a family who will always be there for you."

He raised his glass a bit higher and said, "To Cassidy."

Everyone clinked their glasses together and took a sip. Heath started to sit down and then added, "One more quick toast. This one is to Lydia, who helped make this delicious meal. We're so happy you've joined your sisters at the farm, and I'm especially thankful for your kitchen skills." He took another sip, and everyone murmured their thanks to Lydia.

"Thank you, Heath. It was my pleasure. Now, let's eat," said Lydia, "before it's all cold."

The group lingered over the meal, visiting and laughing between praising Lydia and Heath for the wonderful food.

May gave her high marks for the scones, as did Leland and Heath.

Heath laughed as he finished his. "Honestly, most of the time I've tried any type of floral-flavored foods, they tend to taste like soap, but this is nice, subtle, and the lemon works really well with it."

Micki nodded as she finished her last bite of Heath's casserole. "The scones are delicious. So flaky and just perfect."

Heath grinned. "The secret is keeping the butter cold."

Lydia giggled and choked on her sip of tea. "He's right; that's the secret."

Over the hours, everyone kept nibbling and refilling their plates until all the food was gone. Olivia suggested she take the dogs for a walk, and Leland wanted to go with her. Duke offered to go with them and soon, Clay and Harry were part of the walking group. Micki and Meg thanked Lydia and Heath before leaving for Medford to visit the hospital.

After seeing Micki off, Buck opted to stay for a bit and visit with May, who wasn't yet cleared for walking long distances, and her wrist kept her from doing any lifting. Cassidy insisted on doing the dishes, and Lydia volunteered to help her, with Heath and Buck serving as bus boys and gathering the dishes for them.

Lydia put Cassidy in charge of loading the dishwasher while she tackled some of the bigger pots and pans in the sink. As Cassidy rearranged the plates to squeeze in a few more, she caught Lydia's eye. "Maybe when I come back, you can teach me to make those scones. I eat out most of the time but would love to learn to make a few things."

Lydia squirted soap onto her sponge. "I'd be happy to do that. Your dad, uh, Heath, sorry, is a great cook. He could teach you a few things, too."

She nodded. "Yeah, we were talking about that last night. He said he's not much of a baker and suggested you."

"It sounds like you're definitely coming back to visit. That will make him so happy. He was understandably shocked at first, but I can tell he's delighted to have you here and part of his life." She rinsed a baking sheet. "I never knew my dad, so I understand how important it is."

Cassidy's kind eyes softened. "Thanks for saying that. When my mom told me about Heath, I wasn't sure I believed her. I mean my dad was my dad. None of it made sense, but the idea of having a dad out there kept tugging at me. I wanted to meet him and see if what she said was true. The minute I saw him, I knew it was."

"I'm sorry about the loss of your mom, too. I'm not sure if Heath and Clay told you, but all of us that live at the farm next door, we were all foster children and grew up here. We never met each other, but our foster mom, Jewel, was the absolute best, and she wanted all of us to come back here. She thought we would need our sisters of the heart, that's what she calls us. She wanted us to be a family."

Tears spilled out of Cassidy's beautiful eyes. "That's so sad and sweet at the same time. Heath did mention something about you all being foster sisters. I don't think I realized you hadn't met before. I'm an only child and always wanted a sister or brother."

"Me, too. Now, I have four. One more of us, Georgia, is coming in June. You can meet her when you come back."

She smiled and pulled out the top rack, adding a few more bowls to it. "I'd like that. It's been really hard losing my mom, but I feel better here with all of you. It's like I'm not alone now."

A lump formed in Lydia's throat, and she turned on the faucet. Cassidy's words rang true. It was so nice to feel part of something, a family of sorts. She'd been on her own for so long, Lydia forgot what it was like. She hated thinking she would leave all this soon.

As she rinsed the same pan again and again, she willed her mind to focus on the present and not worry about the future. She couldn't bear to think about the day she'd have to say goodbye.

CHAPTER THIRTEEN

With Monday a holiday, everyone got a later start than usual. Lydia was happy to have a few days off, although her bank account was less thrilled. She was finding a groove at the restaurant and enjoyed being back in a real kitchen. Harry made a trip to town to pick up some pastries from the Sugar Shack, which unlike most businesses, was open. While she was gone, Lydia made another slab of shortbread to go with the strawberries that needed to be eaten.

After they ate, Harry suggested they load up the dogs, take a drive around the property, and visit the lake where Jewel wanted her and Chuck interred. They used the old ranch truck Heath loaned Meg, and she and Olivia rode in the back of the truck with the dogs to make sure they were safe. Lydia kept Vera on her lap in the cab of the truck.

Harry drove slowly, and it took forever to reach the small lake at the edge of the property. The dogs bailed out and ran through the grass and along the edge of the water. As soon as

Lydia placed Vera on the ground, she sprinted for them and joined in the fun.

After they watched the dogs romp for a few minutes, Harry pointed at the big tree that bordered the lake. "Jewel wants us to spread some of their ashes around the farm and then inter them here by the tree. We'll need to get some sort of marker."

Micki looked up at the thick branches of the maple tree. "It's gorgeous, and I remember Jewel always loved it here by the lake. I remember the leaves being a stunning red in the fall."

Olivia joined Micki in gazing at the tree. "We should get a marker ordered, and maybe we can plan a celebration at the end of the festival. Georgia needs to be here, and I think it might be too much to try to squeeze it in before the festival."

They all agreed that sounded like the best timing. Harry volunteered to handle the marker.

Lydia stared at the tree for a few moments. "I think it would be fitting to have a dinner party in the lavender field to say goodbye to Jewel. I'm happy to plan that and put together a menu. We can choose a date when Georgia arrives."

Micki smiled. "That sounds perfect. She was beloved by the entire town, and I'm sure they'll all want to come."

As the women took in the serene beauty of the clear lake and the vibrant green of late spring, they let the dogs wander and sniff to their hearts' content. As the dogs explored, they were drawn to the lake, and the women followed, walking along the edge to keep an eye on their furry family.

Olivia glanced across the still water with the sky and clouds reflected in it. "It's so peaceful and beautiful out here."

Harry skipped a rock across the water. "Very fitting for Jewel's choice of her final resting place with Chuck. I think they spent quite a bit of time out here when they first bought the property."

"I remember a few campouts here with a fire and roasting marshmallows," Olivia said with a smile. "Those were the days."

Lydia pointed at the tree. "I remember walking with Jewel and the dogs. She let me pack us a picnic lunch, and we brought it down here and ate while the dogs played in the water." Tears stung her eyes as she recalled those carefree days.

Meg stood at the edge of the water, looking off at the green hills in the distance. Micki slipped an arm around her daughter's shoulder. "Pretty, huh?"

"Yeah." She sighed. "I wish I could have met Jewel. She sounds like she'd be a great grandma."

Lydia chuckled. "I think you're right, and she had such a true love for children. She had more patience than I do, I know that. She managed everything with such ease. She never got mad or upset and had such a calm way about her. It was reassuring to me."

They all nodded and agreed as they continued to chat and stroll near the edge of the lake.

After letting the dogs swim, except for Vera, who wasn't convinced that was a good idea, they let them sprawl in the sunshine to dry and then loaded them back in the truck for the trip home.

While Lydia went inside to get started on their Monday family dinner, the others stayed out on the back porch and helped Olivia brush the dogs. Vera opted to stay outside with her pack of friends and watch.

Meg changed her clothes and promised to be home before midnight. One of her coworkers invited her to a barbeque for the holiday, and she was excited to go. Micki saw her off and walked into the kitchen on her way back to the porch. "I'm sure she'll have more fun than hanging out with a bunch of old ladies." She chuckled and asked if Lydia needed help.

She waved away her offer. "I've got it handled. Just relax and enjoy yourself." Micki smiled and wandered back to the porch to join the others. Lydia gathered the ingredients she needed for her chicken fettucine with lemon alfredo sauce and eyed the fresh veggies from the farmer's market. She cut up part of a loaf of bread into cubes, drizzled olive oil over them, added salt, and then set them to bake in the oven.

Panzanella was a favorite of all her sisters, and she loved making it. While the croutons were crisping, she cut up tomatoes, red onion, and fresh basil, along with using up the mozzarella balls left in the fridge.

She put together a simple wine vinaigrette with fresh garlic and by the time she was done, the croutons were ready. She let them cool before adding them to the large bowl with the other ingredients.

After dipping a crouton into her dressing to sample both, Lydia turned her attention to getting the water boiling for the pasta. While it heated, she browned the chicken in oil and once done, cut it into strips. Next came the lemon alfredo sauce, which incorporated fresh lemon juice instead of white wine.

It was quick to put together, and she had it ready by the time the pasta was cooked. She tossed the pasta with the creamy sauce and added the strips of crispy chicken on top, squeezing fresh lemon on top.

After adding the croutons to the salad, she tossed it with the dressing and set everything on the table. Lydia washed her hands and wandered to the porch, where all the dogs were asleep.

They sprang to life as soon as she announced dinner was ready. Olivia hurried and made them their bowls, so they could eat and relax while the humans enjoyed Lydia's meal.

The ladies loved the fresh lemon sauce with the chicken, and Lydia didn't have to worry about any leftover panzanella. Harry reached for her iced tea. "I honestly don't know how we survived without you, Lydia. Your food is beyond good."

"You definitely put the rest of us to shame," said Micki.

Olivia chuckled. "And you make it look so easy. I struggle to make the few things I do know how to make."

"Cooking is like an escape for me. I get lost in the moment, and everything fades into the background, except the tasks at hand. I really enjoy it and love being back in a real restaurant."

"You can count us among your biggest fans," said Harry, gathering the empty plates. "It was delicious."

Micki looked at the time. "We better get this cleaned up so we can get online and visit with Georgia."

Lydia sliced the strawberries while the others did all the dishes and tidied the kitchen. When it was time to call Georgia, they gathered around the laptop on the dining room table, beverages next to them.

Micki clicked some keys and moments later, Georgia's smiling face filled the screen. "Oh, I'm so happy to see all your beautiful faces."

Micki glanced over to Lydia. "We have a surprise for you. Lydia arrived, and we just had the most wonderful meal she made for us."

Lydia waved. "Hi, Georgia. I'm anxious to meet you in person."

"Well, I'm so happy you arrived. We were getting worried about you. I'm sure they told you I planned to be there much earlier." She repositioned herself and showcased the sling on her shoulder.

"Yes, I'm sorry you're dealing with that, but you're smart to let it heal."

"I'm just impatient," she said, with a roll of her eyes.

Harry waved at the screen. "Georgia, we were talking about planning a memorial event for Jewel after the festival. Lydia volunteered to plan it and the menu, and I'm going to order a marker. She wants us to scatter some of her and Chuck's ashes around the farm and then place them down by the lake under a tree."

"Oh, that's perfect," said Georgia. "I think I know exactly the spot she's talking about. That huge maple tree, right?"

They nodded. "That's it. I'll get some ideas from the stone mason and email you them, so we can decide together," said Harry.

The conversation drifted to early memories of their time living with Jewel. Harry took a sip of iced tea. "I came to live with Jewel because my parents had died earlier, and I was living with my grandmother, who passed away. That brought me to Jewel, and she reminded me of my grandmother, younger of course, but the same gentle qualities Lydia mentioned. Jewel made a horrible situation much easier and had a way of making me feel important."

Olivia nodded. "Oh, yes, she was very patient. She took so much time with me and let me come along at my own pace. Like so many, my childhood was horrible, and my mother was abusive." She rubbed at her forearm and slid up her sleeve. "The result of her worst abuse is this scar. It's a reminder of what finally brought me here to Jewel's house and although I always tried to hide it, Jewel told me it was a symbol of my strength, not a weakness. Right away, she could tell I connected with her dogs in the rescue, and she trusted me to help care for them. It ignited something inside me and while helping them, I ended up healing my heart."

Her voice cracked, and she reached for her mug of tea. After a few swallows, she continued, "I thought all that despair was behind me until I lost my son and my marriage disintegrated. Coming back here, back to the farm, I found the strength I needed. I credit Jewel for that, too."

Lydia stared at the rough scar on Olivia's arm, and her throat went dry when Olivia mentioned the loss of her son. She put her hand over Olivia's. "I'm so sorry about your son. I can't believe you've been through all that, and you're so kind and happy."

Olivia entwined her fingers with Lydia's. "That's thanks to Jewel and everyone here in Lavender Valley. I wasn't sure I could survive after Simon's death but being here reminded me of everything Jewel stood for and turning my sorrow around to help others, along with the outpouring of love and kindness, helped heal me again."

Lydia swallowed hard. "I was sent here to live with Jewel after my mother killed a man."

Everyone, including Georgia, gasped. Lydia took in their wide eyes and fortified herself with another sip of tea. "My mom was a mess. Drunk most of the time. I never knew my dad. We lived in squalor and filth. I tried to keep my room clean, but she seemed to resent that. Looking back, I'm sure she was an addict. There was a revolving door of men in and out of our house. I never felt safe at home. Mom would fly off the handle and yell and throw things without any provocation. She seemed to have a built-in defect when it came to picking men. When I was too young to understand when she referred to them as uncles, but as I grew older, I realized what they were."

Micki's eyes softened, and her head bobbed as she listened to Lydia.

"Anyway, I hated being there when Mom would bring men around. They were gross, and I did my best to stay away from them. If I did talk to them, Mom would accuse me of being too friendly, like she was jealous or something. They were all scum, except one guy. His name was Tim, and he had gentle eyes and a kind smile. I was hoping he really liked Mom and that maybe we could be a family."

She ran her finger over the rim of her mug. "One afternoon, he came to the door, and Mom was at the store. He asked if he could wait, and I let him. He was asking me about school and what I liked to do. A few minutes later, Mom came home, and I could tell she was angry. She told me to go to my room and in no time, I heard a huge commotion."

She took a long breath and another sip of tea. "I crept out of my room and saw the two of them in the kitchen. Shards of broken dishes littered the floor. Tom was grabbing Mom's wrist, and that's when I noticed she had a big knife. I think he might have heard me because he turned his head, and she broke loose and stabbed him in the chest."

"Oh, my gosh. That had to have been horrible for you to witness," said Harry.

"It was awful. He fell down on the ground, and then she kept stabbing him. There was blood everywhere. I don't remember screaming, but according to the police, that's what triggered our neighbor to call them."

Lydia had never told anyone this story. Her palms were sweaty and despite all the tea, her throat was dry. "They came and took Mom away, and I just remember sitting there on the floor, staring at Tim's blood leaking onto the bits of broken dishes on the dirty floor. I thought he was my chance for a normal family, but that dream died with him."

Tears dotted Micki's cheeks. "Oh, Lydia, I'm so very sorry you had to go through such trauma."

Lydia shrugged. "It was a long time ago. That's how I ended up in the system. I wasn't especially nice to Jewel when I arrived. I was angry and as much as I hated our life, I worried about my mom. She ended up dying in prison. I only saw her once. I never wanted to go back again. As awful as it all was, I was actually relieved and felt safe here at the farm."

Micki refilled Lydia's cup and after another sip, she continued, "Jewel was patient with me, though. She let me explore cooking. Living with Mom, we only had an antenna for our television and didn't get many channels, but I watched the cooking shows on PBS. I only mentioned watching them a few times, and Jewel figured out that might be a way to connect with me. She let me try recipes and make a total mess of her kitchen. I loved cooking and creating and with her help, discovered my passion. It helped me more than the therapists my social worker insisted I see."

Georgia's voice came through the speakers. "Nurturing our passion. That's a common theme for our Jewel. She had a way of figuring out what inspired each of us and nurturing that interest. She was an incredible mother, teacher, and friend. She helped me find my love of sewing and working with yarn. I think so many parents these days try to force their kids into things they like or bounce them from activity to activity, whether it be sports or clubs and often don't take the time to figure out what brings their children true joy and fulfillment. Just listening to your stories makes me realize how selfless Jewel was. She never steered us to her interests, but instead learned about what we liked and then figured out how to help us grow."

Micki chuckled. "I can attest to that. Jewel hated computers, but I had a keen interest in them, and she indulged me and tried her best to learn. Now, my interest in flowers was one she shared, so that was so easy, but looking back, she supported my fascination with technology, when she had zero interest in it. She may not have wanted to know about computers and software, but she always supported me. There are many biological parents who fail to do that."

Lydia glanced around the table at her newfound sisters. "I know without Jewel, my life would have been much different. I credit her for helping me find a way forward after so much chaos and misery."

All the women around the table had Jewel to thank for giving them a second chance and guiding them on a path to success.

Georgia signed off by blowing them all a kiss and promising to see them soon. They said their goodbyes, and Micki closed the laptop. Lydia almost said more but stopped herself. She wasn't sure if she was ready to let them know if her history was an indication, she worried she was like her mother when it came to choosing romantic partners.

CHAPTER FOURTEEN

Lydia spent her days off perfecting a recipe for chocolate truffles infused with lavender, lavender caramels, and honey lavender lollipops. Between cooking, she worked on a few rough menu ideas for Jewel's memorial, took long walks through the fields, and met her sisters for lunch at the deli on Thursday.

They did some window shopping while they were in town, and Olivia talked them all into helping her try out the goat pajamas that arrived in the mail. It had been years since Lydia laughed that hard. It took a few tries and some finessing of their approach to get the wiggly goats into the pajamas. It seemed as soon as they got two legs covered, the goats wrangled out of them. By the time they were done, all of the sisters were covered in dirt, and the pajamas were on but caked with dirt and grass from the wrestling match.

Olivia suggested next time they tackle them one at a time and take them to the backyard or the porch on a leash, where they had a better chance of keeping them clean. She surmised the goats thought it was a game and made the most of teaming up to thwart their opponents. They vowed never to speak of the goats getting the best of them, especially to Heath and Clay, who would no doubt think they were ridiculous.

As Lydia made dinner for everyone on Thursday, she laughed at the memory of the goat circus. She was falling in love with the small town, the farm, the animals, and most of all, her sisters of the heart. Lydia surprised herself by thinking how nice it would be to stay and be surrounded by family. Having their support and friendship lightened her heart, and her normally high level of anxiety had disappeared.

By Friday, she was back at work. With the unofficial start of summer kicking off last weekend with the Memorial Day holiday, the restaurant was filled with people until closing. She didn't even have time for a break and with all the late diners, she got home over an hour later than she expected.

Exhausted, she slept later than usual on Saturday and when she came out from showering in Harry's bathroom, she found her sipping coffee in the kitchen. Micki and Meg were on their way to visit Jade, and Olivia was at Duke's. Hope and Chief lounged on the rug with Vera between them.

Harry smiled at Lydia and slid a gift bag with the logo from Cranberry Cottage on it across the counter. "This is from all of us. We wanted to thank you for your wonderful meals. You've gone above and beyond, so we thought you deserved a token of our appreciation."

Lydia smiled and dug through the tissue paper. She pulled out the gorgeous hydrangea tote bag and the blue hat she'd seen on her first day back in Lavender Valley. "Oh, I love these. How did you know?"

Harry smiled and arched her brows. "A couple of little birds at the store said you'd been looking at them."

"Thank you. That's so generous of all of you. I love them." The sting of tears burned her throat. She glanced at the counter and saw the kettle was still hot. Her vision blurred as tears gathered, and she hurried over to the cupboard for a mug, hoping to focus on a task and squelch them. She didn't need to turn into a blubbering mess.

As she selected a tea bag and poured the water, she blinked and willed herself to pull it together. By the time her tea was ready, her eyes were dry, and she took a quick sip to soothe her throat.

The front gate chimed, and Harry said, "That'll be Clay. We're going to run to Costco and go to lunch."

Lydia brought her cup to the counter and slid into her seat. She admired the tote bag and checked the outer pockets and large zipper middle compartment inside of it. The compartment was big enough to hold everything she could think of, including a change of clothes and toys for Vera. The blue hat would be perfect for spending time outdoors at the festival.

Harry answered the knock on the door and led Clay and Heath to the kitchen. Heath held a newspaper in his hand and slid it over to Lydia. His smile stretched all the way to his eyes. "Figured you hadn't seen the paper yet."

She frowned and took the paper. As she read the headline, she dropped her mug and spilled hot tea all over the counter. Her mouth hung open.

Harry rushed to grab a towel to mop up the mess.

"What's wrong, Lydia?" Heath bent down to get in her line of vision. "Are you okay?"

She pointed at the paper. The words were stuck in her throat, and panic bubbled to the surface. "Who, who did this?"

Heath reached for her hand. "Curt, he's the local editor of

the paper and writes most of the articles. He's a good guy. What's wrong, Lydia?"

She shook her head as she skimmed the story. Her eyes wouldn't focus beyond the headline. FORMER PORTLAND BAKE-OFF WINNER IS NEW CHEF AT THE RANCH HOUSE.

Her hands shook as she saw her name in the first paragraph. Her stomach fell, and her heart beat faster. "I need to leave. I can't stay here."

Think, Lydia. Think. Where can I go? Like she'd done so many times before, she would set out on the road and choose a direction when she got to the highway. One thing she knew, she needed to get out of Oregon.

Lost in her own thoughts, she didn't notice Heath's hands on her shoulders. "Lydia, Lydia, what do you mean?"

Harry moved to the dining table. "Sit down and tell us what's wrong. Maybe we can help you. You're scared of something, just tell us."

Lydia's hands shook as she let Heath lead her to the chair next to Harry's. "It's a long story. An embarrassing one." All three dogs rushed over to surround Lydia, and Vera stood on her hind legs, begging to be held. Lydia picked her up and set her in her lap, stroking her soft ears.

Heath put a hand on her shoulder. "Like as embarrassing as having the daughter you never knew show up thirty years later? Trust me, you can't top that one."

She appreciated his effort at humor, but her stomach roiled. "I feel sick," she said, putting her hand on her midsection.

Clay looked toward the fridge. "You need some ginger ale." He and Heath hurried to the kitchen.

Lydia shut her eyes and stifled a sob. Harry patted her hand. "Just relax. Breathe in. One. Two. Three. Four. Now out." Hope leaned her head against Lydia's thigh and kept it there. Lydia reached out and put her hand on the dog's head.

After a few deep breaths, her heart rate slowed. Clay brought a tall glass filled with ice and ginger ale and brought a fresh pot of tea to the table, along with four cups. She took a small sip of the cool ginger ale and let the bubbles dance across her tongue and down her throat.

"I've been hiding from my ex for years. I move around and stay off the grid as much as possible." She stifled a sob and willed herself to swallow the bile rising in her throat.

"It started a few years ago. I was working a private event for a politician in Portland. He was running for reelection, and everybody who was anybody was there. The food was exquisite, and I was in my element, as far as that went. It was the typical hobnobbing of the rich and important class. I was being paid well and focused on the food, making sure everything went smoothly."

She took another swallow from her glass. Her stomach settled a bit. "I was one of the last to leave the venue. It was at somebody's huge waterfront mansion in Lake Oswego. Beyond gorgeous views, a pool, lots of outdoor entertainment space. A bit too modern for my tastes but a great venue. Anyway, this guy, who turned out to be the chief of staff for the senator running in the election, comes up to me and tells me how wonderful the food was and that he was so impressed, and he has many friends, and he would be happy to recommend me to them for future jobs."

She stared at a bubble in her glass and watched it rise from the bottom of the glass, move up, and escape when it reached the top. "That was the first time I met Marcus. Marcus Blackwood." She shivered as his name left her lips.

"As he promised, he recommended me to others in his connected and exclusive circle. I made good money and the more events I did, the more I booked. I became sought after in the exclusive clique of the rich and powerful. Things went along like that for several months."

Heath poured himself a cup of tea. "Marcus sounds like a real tool already."

Lydia hung her head. "I wish I was as perceptive as you." She took the cup of tea Heath offered. "Looking back, I can see how he manipulated me and drew me into his nasty web. He called me and invited me to a symphony. He wanted to thank me for catering a last-minute function the senator had and said he could introduce me to some people who were looking for someone to cater a holiday party."

Hope moved her head and slithered down to the floor next to Lydia's feet, where Chief was resting. "I was enjoying the extra income from all the work Marcus was shoving my way, so I went. I bought a new dress since I didn't have anything worthy of the symphony. Thank goodness I found something at a consignment shop. Marcus was a perfect gentleman, and I forgot to mention he was tall and handsome, always impeccably dressed, and very polite." She shook her head. "It hid the ugliness underneath."

Harry, who always seemed to have a pen and notepad handy, scribbled notes as Lydia told her story. "As time went on, we went out a few more times. Again, it was enjoyable and nice. A little out of my element but fun in an almost fairytale kind of way. I could never afford the places we went, and he knew everyone and was suave and polished."

She traced her finger down the side of her glass, wiping away the condensation. "Things escalated from there, and we were going out at least once a week and getting more serious romantically. He had a nice house in Portland Heights and worked in the senator's downtown office. I also made lots of trips to Salem with him. I was dumb enough to get swept up in that lifestyle. One I'd never experienced and only read about or saw from behind my apron when I was serving the affluent class."

She shook her head. "I'm not proud of that. I let it override that little voice in the back of my head that kept telling me something wasn't right. I figured that out the first time I said no to Marcus. He wanted me to go somewhere, and I had to work. He was mad and acted like a real jerk, but he later apologized with flowers and a special dinner and a bracelet."

Harry nodded. "He sounds like a skilled abuser."

"Right. It was a pattern. Each time I couldn't go somewhere with him or couldn't cater some event he thought he could just spring on me at the last minute, or I simply didn't want to go, he became outraged. He'd grab me by the upper arms and squeeze so hard, it would leave bruises. It brought back lots of bad memories with my mom. So, I tried not to irritate him, but at the same time, I tried to distance myself."

After a few more swallows of ginger ale, she continued, "This dance went on for months. He'd get mad and then come begging for forgiveness with expensive gifts. I finally had enough and told him it was over. That sent him into a rage like I've never seen. He told me someone like me couldn't treat him like that, and I could never leave him. He said he'd kill me if I tried to leave. He chuckled like a horrible comic villain. He slammed me against the wall and choked me. So hard, I thought he was going to kill me right then. I had bruises for a week and had to hide them with turtlenecks. I was scared and mortified. Not to mention, stuck."

Lydia ran her hands over Vera. "I was living in an apartment with a roommate. I focused on working as much as I could, using that as an excuse to not see Marcus as much as possible, but I also wanted to appear normal and compliant. He made a point of telling me again he'd kill me before he ever let me leave him and that nobody left Marcus Blackwood."

Harry shook her head in disgust. "I'd socked away a bunch of money and when the legislative session started, and I knew he'd be gone for several days, I drove my old car to Vancouver, Washington and sold it at one of those cash lots. I found Gypsy on Craig's List and bought it for cash. A classmate from culinary school lived in Washington and was willing to let me use her address. I got a driver's license and registered the motorhome there. I wanted to disappear and didn't want to have anything to do with Oregon, where I knew Marcus had connections."

Harry tapped her pen on her notepad. "I assume he has friends in the police?"

Lydia nodded. "Oh, yeah. I didn't trust anyone in Oregon. I did end up working at a café in Brookings for a time. I stuck to small towns far away from Salem, Eugene, or Portland, where the senator had field offices. I worked for cash if I could or traded my services for a place to park Gypsy and my utilities and food. I moved often, figured out how to use burner phones, and changed them out every few weeks. I never told my roommate or my friend in Washington where I was going. I just disappeared."

Harry looked up from her notes. "Did Marcus know about Jewel or your time here in Lavender Valley?"

Lydia shook her head. "I never told him. He didn't ask much about me beyond me telling him my mom was dead, and I never knew my dad. He was very self-absorbed. I was worried though that he might find out or pull my records or something. That's part of the reason I stayed away from here and Jewel. I didn't want to bring trouble. My friend handles my registration and insurance for me, and I just send her money orders to cover the costs. I used to check in with her more often to make sure nobody was snooping around, and I always toss my phone after I talk to her."

Heath turned to her. "That's no way to live, Lydia. You shouldn't be the one running and afraid because of this bastard." He reached over and squeezed her hand in his.

Tears leaked from her eyes. She'd been keeping this horrible secret to herself for so long, the strength of his hand on hers was overwhelming. It meant so much, but she didn't want to risk the safety of any of her sisters. Marcus was violent and unpredictable, and she would never forgive herself if he hurt them.

Harry nodded. "He's right. This has gone on long enough. You don't need to run. We can help you and protect you." She asked Lydia a few more details, including the name of the senator. "At best, Marcus is a domestic abuser, but it sounds like he's more of a narcissistic psychopath."

Lydia's eyes widened. "That's exactly what I thought. I went to the library to research and came up with that diagnosis. Behind his charming façade, he's a manipulator with a strong need for admiration and control."

Harry's eyes narrowed. "No more running, Lydia. This is your home, and we're your family. One way or another, we'll handle this guy. He's just another scummy perp, dressed up nice and pretty, but he's a common thug."

Clay smiled and put an arm around Harry's shoulders. "She's right, and you've got all of us on your side, Lydia. Don't be afraid anymore. Like Heath said, you can't keep living like this."

Heath squeezed her hand again. "I know one thing, there's no way you're staying alone in that motorhome of yours. We've got a house full of guest rooms, and one of them is yours, until this is over. Or we can have Meg or Micki stay at the ranch, and you can stay in the house, whatever is easiest."

His eyes searched for his brother's. Clay nodded. "Yes, whatever we need to do, we'll do it. We've been lax with the gate, but we can lock it down, like you've done here when Jade arrived and harassed Micki. Whatever makes you feel safe." He leaned against Harry. "With Harry on your side, you don't need to worry. I can already see her wheels turning, and she's an excellent shot."

Harry grimaced. "Hopefully, it won't come to that." She tapped her pen on her notepad. "I've got an idea. I need to make some calls and look into our friend, Marcus."

Heath sputtered. "Marcus. Even his name sounds like a jackass."

CHAPTER FIFTEEN

Heath volunteered or rather insisted he stay and keep an eye on Lydia while Clay and Harry made their Costco run.

Lydia couldn't sit still and slipped on an apron and rummaged through the cupboards. Heath sat at the counter, sipping some iced tea. "What are you making?"

"Just a chocolate cake. Baking calms me when I'm stressed." She scooped flour out of the canister while the dogs settled on the rug to watch.

"Sounds good to me," said Heath.

"I should probably call Cyrus and let him know I can't work. This is all such a mess."

He frowned. "We don't know that Marcus knows you're here. Our local paper is not exactly a highly circulated publication."

She shrugged. "I think it's only a matter of time. Like hours or days. I'm sure he has one of those alerts for my name, and it will pick it up soon."

"I could take you to work and pick you up. That way you'd never be alone."

She shook her head. "I don't know." She hated being a burden, and tears clouded her eyes. She blinked several times as she mixed the batter. "I resent the fact that I even have to think about Marcus. I feel like a mouse waiting for him to pounce on me."

"You deserve the life you want, not one running from some creep or worrying about him constantly. Living in fear is not really living, Lydia. You've been surviving, existing, but not truly living or flourishing. Together, we're going to strip him of this power he has over you. He's a punk and needs a dose of reality. If he tries anything around here, he'll get a good ass kicking."

Lydia grinned as she poured the smooth batter into pans and put them in the oven. "I'd like to see that."

"Don't you think you've given up enough of your happiness? Between all of us, we can watch over you and keep you safe until we get this whole thing handled. If you like working at the Ranch House, you need to keep working there. No more moving and running. You're not alone anymore, and I understand not wanting to ask for help, but you don't even need to ask. I want you to be safe and happy."

She smiled softly, while warmth spread through her chest. She'd never had a man care for her like this. She felt safe around Heath, like she could trust him with anything. He was a good man.

Unlike Marcus, who sought out her vulnerabilities and preyed upon her, always looking for ways to manipulate. At the time, she wrote it off to his job and profession. Politics was filled with vipers, and everything seemed to work on a transactional basis. He lived in an entirely different world and while she'd been impressed with the lavishness and beauty, it only served to hide his dark self. Nothing was real, pure, and good in his world. Everything and everyone had a price. Now, she saw Marcus for what he was.

Heath was the antithesis of Marcus and everything he was. No suit and tie, no perfect hair, no fancy job, no circle of friends who dined with senators, no fake charm. With Heath, what you saw was what you got. She ventured to guess Heath had far more material wealth than Marcus, but Heath never flaunted it. Never treated others poorly or beneath him. He was a man she could count on and would be there for his friends and family.

She'd seen him vulnerable when Cassidy showed up out of the blue. He didn't pretend and hide behind a veneer. He was real and let her see his pain. That signaled trust.

She trusted him, too. The flutter in her chest told her it was something more than trust. More than friendship.

By the time Harry and Clay returned, Lydia was resolved to continuing at the restaurant and having Heath serve as her personal bodyguard and chauffer. Lydia helped Harry put their groceries away while Heath and Clay waited at the table with the promise of chocolate cake.

Harry restocked their coffee beans and turned to Lydia. "I'm glad you're going to keep working. I've dealt with issues like this several times, and I've already got some people I trust looking into a few things. Just promise me, until this is resolved, you won't go anywhere alone. I think the idea of staying at the ranch is a solid one. I know you're independent and would rather we weren't all involved in your business, but I have a gut feeling about this guy, and it's not good."

Lydia nodded. "I admit, it's embarrassing, but the more Heath talked, the more it made sense. I can't keep doing this, and he told me I deserve to be happy and have the life I want." Her voice cracked. "Outside of Jewel, nobody has ever said anything like that to me. Not any man, that's for sure."

She shrugged. "After my dismal relationship track record and then this whole ordeal with Marcus, I've stayed far away from anything that resembles a date or serious relationship. I just don't have the energy for it, and I don't trust myself. I've made too many bad choices."

Harry laughed as they carried more staples to the pantry to mudroom. "I hear ya. I'd resolved myself to being alone for the rest of my life." She smiled and gestured with her head toward the dining room. "Then, I met Clay, and he was different. I think I struggled with being weak or thought of as weak if I were with a man. Turns out, I just hadn't met the right one. Clay and I make each other better, stronger. Trust doesn't come easily for me, and I trust Clay with my life."

They walked the empty boxes outside. Harry caught Lydia's eye. "You can trust Heath. He's a good guy. Like Clay, he's honest, hardworking, and trustworthy. He's a man of his word."

Lydia smiled. "I could tell that. He's been more than kind to me, and his willingness to help touches me. I think I'm worried I'll appear weak, sort of like what you were saying. I need to get over that and realize I have a family now... and friends I can count on."

Harry put an arm around her shoulder. "Yes, you do. I'm going to Salem and dig into some of my suspicions. I'm meeting with some old work colleagues, and we have lots of connections in Marcus' world. I'm going to get to the bottom of this and if I'm right, I don't think you're going to have to worry about him ever again."

Lydia couldn't help herself. She wrapped her arms around Harry and hugged her. "Thanks, Harry. You don't understand how much it means to have someone in my corner."

Harry took a few minutes and explained what she wanted to do, and Lydia agreed. They walked back through the mudroom door, and Harry tilted her head toward Heath. "I'm not the only one in your corner."

As the four of them indulged in cake, Olivia came through the door with Willow, along with Micki and Meg. Within a few minutes, Buck and Duke arrived. Everyone gathered in the dining room, and Lydia served up more slices of her delicious cake, covered in a fudgy frosting.

Heath helped her dispense hot tea, iced tea, and coffee around the table. Harry cleared her throat and looked across at Lydia, who dipped her head in a nod. "I called an impromptu family meeting and wanted to explain the situation with Lydia." She went over the facts and Lydia's history with Marcus, much like she were in a police briefing and let the others know the situation with Marcus and Lydia's fears about him targeting her now that the newspaper article was out in the public realm.

"Heath and Clay are going to serve as security for Lydia until we can get this resolved. She's going to stay in one of their guestrooms, and they'll handle getting her to and from work. I've already talked to Chief Phillips about the situation, and he's alerted law enforcement and shared Marcus' information. I wanted everyone to understand the serious nature of this as I believe Lydia isn't the first woman he has abused. It's important to be vigilant about keeping the gate locked and the doors to the house secured."

Lydia took a deep breath. "I'm truly sorry for bringing all of this to your doorstep. I've been running from Marcus for several years and at this point, I don't know if he'll come, if he'll send someone, or if he's moved on and will ignore me entirely. I'm beyond embarrassed to share all this with you, but Harry assured me you're all willing to help and that Marcus needs to be stopped. So, I'm willing to do whatever it takes to put an end to it. As someone reminded me today, I deserve a happy life, and this is my first step." She noticed Heath's slow smile.

Micki leaned over and hugged her. "Yes, you do. We're all here to help and do whatever it takes."

Everyone murmured their support, and Buck was busy taking notes on his legal pad.

Through a few tears, Lydia grinned and laughed with Olivia and Micki, who did their best to cheer her up and reassure her. "Dinner at the ranch Monday night for everyone. It's the least I can do to show my appreciation."

Olivia volunteered to take care of Vera and keep her with her dog friends at the farm so Lydia wouldn't have to worry about her on days she worked.

After listening to the two of them talk about logistics, Heath tapped his fingers on the table. "We can just use the pasture gate to go between both properties. That will keep anyone outside the gates from watching our activity. Clay and I can get the UTV out of the barn and park it out here so it's easy to use. We can show you all how to drive it. It's easy."

Harry explained she was going to head up to Salem as soon as she packed a bag and spend tomorrow there and would have more information when she got home but wanted everyone to stay at home as much as possible. "Chief

Phillips is going to let a few people in town know if they see Marcus or if anyone comes around asking about Lydia to alert his office. That way, we'll have advance notice of any trouble. Nobody lets anyone in the gate. We need to be locked down for the time being and although Lydia is the one Marcus is interested in, he could use any of us to get to her, so I suggest nobody go anywhere alone. While I'm away, Clay will stay here, and he'll let Tyler know what's going on."

Duke nodded. "I'll be sure to service the farm and ranch myself and leave Kyle at the clinic. I think it's wise to limit the traffic while you're figuring things out." He turned toward Micki. "Meg could stay at May's place until this is sorted. That way, you wouldn't have to worry about her being on her own or coming and going for work."

Micki glanced over at her daughter. "I think that might be a good idea. I'm sure May and Leland could keep you busy when you're not working at the clinic."

"Oh, yeah," Meg said with a happy smile. "I'll go pack a bag."

"Speaking of bags to pack," Harry rose from her seat. "I'm going to grab a few things and hit the road. I'll have my cell phone if you need me."

After adding another note, Buck looked up. "I'm going to help Harry out with some investigative work into Marcus, so I need to get back to the office. If you need anything at all, Lydia, just call me."

"Thanks, Buck. I appreciate that." He left Micki with a quick peck on her cheek and said goodbye. Clay and Heath followed him to get the UTV from the barn.

Duke's phone chimed and after a quick conversation, he slipped it in his pocket. "I need to get to the clinic. An emergency is coming in. See you all Monday night if not before." He hugged Olivia and made her promise to be watchful.

Micki hollered at Meg to get a move on so she could follow Duke to the clinic. She hugged her daughter and watched as she hurried to the old truck Heath let her use.

Lydia waved to Duke and Meg and turned to Micki. "With all this ruckus, I forgot to ask about Jade."

Olivia poured more water over her tea bag. "They moved her to a rehab facility late yesterday. She's getting settled, so it was a long day of waiting while they did things. It seems like a nice place. They finally got her health coverage figured out, so that will make things easier. She's going to have to work to regain her strength and the use of her leg and arms."

She sighed. "Meg's worried about where she'll go when she gets out of rehab."

Olivia frowned. "Still no sign she's remembering anything?"

"That's the thing. I saw something flicker in her eyes today. I think Jade does remember. She's pretending not to." With exasperation, Micki rolled her eyes.

Olivia's brows arched. "It might make sense for you to visit her without Meg one day and see if you can have a frank conversation. I could come with you if it would help."

Micki used her fork to scrape up the last bit of frosting from her plate. "That's so sweet of you and a good idea. I'm sure it would be easier for her to pretend the past didn't exist. I also hope Meg is back at school by the time Jade is released. She'll be facing an arrest and then who knows what. I already told her Jade wasn't coming here, but Meg has such a soft spot for her."

Olivia collected the empty plates from the table. "I doubt Lavender Valley has many resources for people in need of housing. I would think Medford might."

Micki nodded, and she and Lydia helped gather empty glasses and cups and load the dishwasher. The dogs wandered over from their rug to prewash anything that needed it. "I asked the social worker at the rehabilitation center to see if she could help find anything for her. I know she was using drugs before the accident. They're giving her stuff for the pain, but I suspect as they cut back on that, Jade will struggle."

Olivia rinsed her hands in the sink. "As bad as it sounds, that might help with regard to finding her some type of group home. There are more resources for addicts sometimes."

Micki blew out a breath. "It's really hard because I don't want anything to do with her, and I know how horrible that sounds, but I need her out of my life. No job, no house, no car. It's not looking good for her to leave the area anytime soon. Honestly, I'm not sure she's ever actually had a job." She chuckled and added, "I'd buy her a used car if it meant she'd leave."

Lydia added detergent to the dishwasher and set it to clean. "Portland and Eugene would have more resources, but more people vying for them, too. Plus, there's a chance she'd relapse and fall in with the wrong people there. Homelessness and drugs are widespread, especially in Portland."

After filling the kettle with water, Olivia leaned against the counter. "Maybe this will be the wake-up call Jade needs, and she'll make some good decisions to get her life on the right path."

Micki sighed. "I hope you're right, but at this point, it's hard to have a positive outlook."

Heath came through the front door. "We've got the UTV ready. We can give you a quick lesson."

Lydia glanced at the clock. "I need to be quick and then pack a few things so I can get organized and get to work."

It only took Heath a few minutes to demonstrate how things worked in the UTV. It was simple, and all of them were confident they could handle driving it, since it was almost as easy as a car. Micki was the first to volunteer to drive it and, after a loop around the barn, parked it close to the mudroom door.

Lydia hurried to her motorhome and packed up her toiletries and clothes. She couldn't resist using her new hydrangea tote bag and even added the blue hat. She made sure to take the hangers holding her uniforms for work, her knife roll, and her good shoes. Olivia helped haul Vera's toys and her fluffy bed and brought them into the house.

Heath opened the passenger door of Clay's truck and helped Lydia get her things situated in the back of the truck and retrieved Clay's duffel and left it on the porch.. While they were doing that, Harry came through the front door, toting her overnight bag.

Clay walked her to her SUV, and Lydia smiled as she watched them embrace and Clay kiss her before she slid behind the wheel. With a wave, Harry headed down the driveway.

Lydia promised she'd be right back and darted up the porch. She found Vera nestled with the other dogs, while Micki and Olivia sat at the dining room table, sipping fresh cups of tea. Lydia bent down and snuggled Vera close to her. "You be a good girl. I'll see you tomorrow, sweet one."

"She'll be fine. We'll take good care of her," said Olivia, walking over to give all of the dogs a bit of attention.

Micki rose and hugged her closely. "You be careful and don't take any chances. Let Heath take care of you and check in and let us know how things are going."

"I will. I'll talk to you tomorrow." Lydia gave Vera a kiss on top of her head and stepped onto the porch, where Clay was coming up the steps.

"You take care of my brother, now." He grinned. He pointed at the door. "I'm going to see if the ladies are up for a game of poker."

Lydia laughed and hurried to the truck, where Heath was waiting for her. Despite the threat of Marcus, for the first time in a long time, she felt like she was home.

CHAPTER SIXTEEN

After a luxurious shower late Monday morning, Lydia padded down the long hallway from Heath's wing of the house to the kitchen. The smell of fresh coffee piqued her interest, and she found Heath seated at the counter, sipping a cup. Maverick and Ace, resting at his feet, perked their ears as they watched her.

"Morning," she said, filling a mug of her own.

"How'd you sleep?"

"Great. This place is like a five-star hotel." She chuckled and waved her hand around the space. "Actually, much better since I have access to this awesome kitchen. I'm also relieved I'm off for a few days and don't have to worry while I'm at work or have you disrupting your day to watch over me."

He took another swallow from his cup and smiled at her. His blue eyes sparkled in the morning light. "I'm happy to watch over you. I'm glad we haven't seen hide nor hare of Marcus, although I have to admit, I wouldn't mind running into him and giving him a dose of his own medicine. I wandered down Main Street and around the town square while you were working and didn't see anyone out of the ordinary."

Marcus and Heath were about the same height, but her money was on Heath if the two of them ever met. Heath was stockier and wrestled with cows most days. She was sure he would have no problem with Marcus. "I'm glad Cheryl and Cyrus were so understanding about it. Cheryl assured me nobody has called or been in asking about me, so that's a relief."

"I talked to Clay this morning, and Harry will be home by late afternoon and will have an update. He set up some trail cameras around the property yesterday, so he's got eyeballs on the most obvious entry points."

"She's really something. She leaps into action and has a plan figured out before I can even think about it." Lydia cradled the warm cup in her hands.

He grinned. "She is something. She helped us win the trophy in our annual shooting contest we hold and brought down our corrupt mayor. I wouldn't want to tangle with her and with all her time working in Salem, I'm sure she's got some great connections when it comes to scum like Marcus."

"She and Clay are so cute together, too." Lydia smiled and went to retrieve the pot of coffee.

He extended his cup. "Harry's the best thing that's happened to Clay since he lost his wife. Honestly, I didn't think he'd ever find someone. Between losing our mom and her, he was broken. When she moved in next door, it was like a light turned on inside of him. He's much more relaxed and smiles all the time."

"I know Harry thinks the world of Clay."

"He's the best man I know. The best brother a man could have."

"I sure appreciate both of you going to all this trouble for me."

He grinned. "It's no trouble. It's what you do for someone you care about."

She took another sip from her cup, hoping to hide the heat in her cheeks. "I should start the sauce for the pasta, and then I thought I'd sneak over to pick up Vera and bring her over, if that's okay?"

"Of course. She's welcome anytime." Heath gestured toward the cabinets. "We've got toast, oatmeal, cereal, some fruit. Just help yourself. I was up early and ate already."

"Thanks, I'll make some toast. Did you get the steak marinating for your kabobs?"

He saluted her. "Yes, Chef. I just need to cut up the veggies later and put them on the grill."

She laughed at his antics. "The garlic bread won't take long, and we've got the stuff for a salad. What about dessert?"

"That chocolate cake you made went over well. We've got some ice cream in the freezer to go with it."

"Sold. I'll have a bit of breakfast and get cracking."

It didn't take her long to brown the ground beef and sausage and combine the other ingredients to make the sauce. As she was in the middle of it, Heath's phone rang.

He smiled and said, "Hey, Cassidy." He and the dogs wandered out to the patio and as she finished the sauce, her heart warmed to hear his laughter.

With the sauce done, she turned her attention to the cake and by the time Heath was off the phone, she had it in the oven and two iced teas poured for them. He slid into a chair at the counter. "That sauce smells delicious."

"How's Cassidy?"

"Fine. She's coming to the festival, shooting for mid-July. She's going to check her schedule and let me know for sure."

"Wow, that's great. It's nice that she wants to stay connected and come to see you. I'm sure it's hard for her to be alone after losing her mom and then have everything she thought was true, turn out to be something else."

He nodded. "She's got a deep love for her mom and her dad, but I think she might feel a little betrayed, but she feels guilty for being upset."

"That makes sense. I carried guilt about my mom for a very long time. Angry and embarrassed, too. Not too many teenagers can say their mother killed a man in front of them."

Heath's eyes went wide. "Oh, wow. That's horrible, Lydia. I'm so sorry."

She shook her head. "It was a long time ago, and I'm over it. Jewel was the one who helped me see through the anger and shame. My mom was a complete loser and ironically, she killed the one normal guy she brought home. All the others were total scum. I felt so sorry for him and as much as I despised her and hated the way we lived, when she went to jail, my heart sank. Not so much for her, but because I knew I had nowhere to go and would be at the mercy of the system."

"I'm just glad you were placed with Jewel."

"At the time, I was scared and angry, but it didn't take long for Jewel to win me over and for me to realize I'd finally found a real home. Chuck and Jewel were the best. They helped heal my heart and taught me I was worth something."

He reached across the counter for her hand. "Somehow, I think Jewel knew you needed to be here. Back at the farm again."

Along with the rich scent of her sauce simmering, the enticing aroma of warm chocolate filled the air. Lydia smiled as she relished in the comfort of his hand over hers. She studied his hand, with its nicks and cuts. It wasn't smooth and refined, nor was it small. The roughness of his skin against hers didn't bother her. It was the hand of a working man, a protector.

The timer dinging interrupted her thoughts. She took the cake out, this one in a Bundt pan, and set it to cool. Heath found a glass cake plate and set it on the counter. "This was my mom's favorite."

She fingered the blush-colored Depression glass plate elevated on a small pedestal. "It's lovely. I'll be very careful with it."

He grinned. "I trust you completely."

She used a silicone spatula and tested pulling the edges away from the pan. As she removed the cake, Heath's phone rang again.

"Hey, Micki. Everything okay?"

Lydia situated the cake and set the pan aside before rushing to the counter, fear knotting her stomach.

"Oh, yeah, that sounds good and makes sense. We'll come over and pick up Vera in a few minutes." He smiled at Lydia and gave her a thumbs up.

Relief flooded through her, and she went back to the sink to wash the pan.

Heath carried his empty cup to the sink. "Micki said Olivia is willing to go with her to see Jade and evaluate her without Meg there. They want to go while Meg is away but didn't want to leave the farm if we thought it was a bad idea. Clay's going to stay there and monitor things. We can run over and pick up Vera."

She glanced at the clock, surprised it was a few minutes past noon. "I'm ready anytime you are."

He let Maverick and Ace know they'd be right back and

led the way to the back of the house and the waiting UTV. He urged Lydia to drive so she could practice and after a bit of coaxing, she settled in and followed the path to the gate between the property.

He hopped out and opened the gate, closing it behind her, and they made their way to the house. As she drove by the lavender fields, she noticed a few bursts of purple blooms that had appeared in the last few days. The lovely scent filled the air and made her think of Jewel. They found Micki and Olivia gathering their things and Vera beyond excited to see Lydia. Her little bum wouldn't stop wiggling.

Micki gestured toward her SUV. "We won't be long. I think Jade is remembering and faking it now. I'd like to have a frank conversation with her, and Olivia is going to help."

Lydia hugged her. "I hope it goes well. Be sure to call us when you get there and when you leave, so we know when to expect you."

Olivia nodded. "Will do." She leaned down and petted the three goldens and gave Vera a quick rub on her head. "We won't make any stops other than the rehab center, and Clay has the address."

Heath held the door for them. "I'll just follow you down in the truck to make sure nobody is lurking around and watching." He turned toward Lydia. "Be right back."

She got down on the floor with the dogs and gave them all belly rubs, while Vera curled into her lap. As she massaged Hope's paws, she glanced over at Clay, who was monitoring the trail cameras on his phone. "Thank you for staying here and for letting me stay at the ranch. I hate being the cause of all this trouble and wasting your time."

He wandered into the kitchen and poured a cup of coffee for each of them. "You're not the cause of it. Marcus is the culprit, and men like him need to be stopped. If I can help bring a measure of justice to the world, I'm always happy to. The minute Harry heard your story, I saw her wheels turning. She's onto something, and I have a hunch she's going to get to the bottom of it. She's the most determined woman I've ever met."

She noticed his grin when he mentioned Harry and the pride in his tone. "I would agree with that. I'm grateful she's willing to help. With Marcus' connections, it makes it really hard to even think of asking for help. He delights in using his power to get what he wants, at any cost."

With a tilt of his head, Clay said, "I doubt he's ever met anyone like Harry. She doesn't care about connections or political pressure or whatever power he thinks he has. She'll delight in taking him down."

Heath drove up to the house and minutes later, came through the door. "Anything?" Clay asked.

He shook his head and leaned against the counter. "I didn't see anyone and stayed and watched until they drove out of sight, just to make sure someone wasn't hiding in the trees and waiting."

Clay nodded and finished his coffee. "We haven't noticed anything unusual here. Nothing on the cameras. So far, so good."

Lydia untangled herself from the dogs and stood. "We should probably get back so I can check on my sauce."

Clay pointed out the window. "I'm going to have Tyler come up to the house and keep an eye on things while we gather at the ranch tonight. We'll come over as soon as Harry gets home."

Heath bent and picked up Vera. Her pink tongue, wet with slobber, darted out and licked his hand. "She's so tiny. I've never been a little dog person, but gotta admit, she's a cutie." He held her against his chest. "Our chariot awaits, my lady."

Lydia laughed and led the way to the UTV. They waved at Clay, who stood on the porch and watched as she drove along the pathway leading to the gate.

A few minutes later, they were back in the kitchen, where Ace and Maverick were anxious to welcome Vera with lots of sniffing and a few licks. Heath watched over them while Lydia stirred the sauce.

After tasting it and finding it needing nothing, she asked for Heath's help in finding the baking dishes. "I think I'm going to go ahead and put this together now. I can pop it in the oven when we're ready to eat. I don't want to be distracted when Harry gets here and tells us the latest."

He found two large baking dishes for her and filled a stock pot with water. She tilted her head toward the refrigerator. "I can help you cut up the veggies and get your kabobs ready for the grill, too. I've just got to put together a salad and get the garlic bread ready. That way all the prep will be done."

"Sounds good." He washed his hands and took out the red and orange peppers and brought the steel skewers and a couple of red onions from the pantry. While he was getting the cutting boards, she dumped the penne pasta into the boiling water and set a timer.

She cut the red pepper into chunks before the timer prompted her to drain the pasta and rinsed it in cold water. She mixed it with the fragrant, thick sauce and stirred it well, making sure all the pasta was coated with sauce. Then, she went about layering it in the bottom of the baking pans, adding shredded mozzarella, slices of provolone, and a bit of sour cream. More pasta covered that, topped with mozzarella and a bit of parmesan cheese. She covered it with foil and popped it in the fridge.

By the time she went back to the island to help with the kabobs, Heath had the onions and remaining peppers cut, and they worked together to add the cubes of marinated steak and the veggies to the skewers.

As they finished them, Heath stacked them in a long roasting pan. "These don't take long to grill, just ten or fifteen minutes."

"The baked penne will take about an hour, since it's in the fridge." She glanced over at the dogs, the three of them snoozing together, with Vera nestled between the two big dogs.

He covered the kabobs and added them to the fridge before cleaning up the counter. While he started the dishes, she put together a chocolate ganache glaze and drizzled it over the cake.

Heath couldn't resist running a finger along the edge of the mixing bowl. He licked it clean and grinned. "That's so good. I'm getting hungry with all this cooking we're doing."

"Oh, I brought home leftovers from work last night. We could have them." She gestured toward the fridge as she finished the cake and added her bowl and utensils to the sink.

He opened the takeout box and wiggled his brows at her. "Honey garlic salmon. Yum."

They worked together to make the salad for dinner and added a good-sized helping of it to two plates. She topped it with the salmon and made a lemon vinaigrette dressing for it.

As they took their first bites of their lunch, Heath groaned. "That is beyond delicious. I thought I was a good cook, but I could get used to eating like this every day."

Her chest fluttered. If he only knew how much she enjoyed today. She loved sharing a kitchen and cooking with him. When he was around, something clicked inside of her. She could get used to this, but she was too scared to say all of that aloud.

CHAPTER SEVENTEEN

The chime of Heath's phone woke them from their after-lunch nap. They and the dogs were sprawled across the couch in the den, where they'd been watching a movie before they fell asleep.

After a quick conversation, he glanced over at her. "Harry's home, and they'll all be here within the hour." He urged the dogs from the couch and reached out his hand to help her from it.

She held his hand even after she was standing. She noticed he didn't pull away either. They wandered down the hallway, still holding hands, and he stopped at the archway that led to the formal dining room.

"With as many people as we have coming, we should probably eat in here."

She nodded. "That works for me. We can set the table and have it ready before they get here."

They worked together and made quick work of putting out placemats, dishes, and silverware. Before they decided to watch a movie, Heath brewed a pitcher of iced tea, filled the kettle, and readied the coffee maker, while Lydia made fresh lemonade.

The granite counter held a variety of glasses and cups. Heath added ice to a bucket while Lydia pushed the button to brew the coffee and added the pitchers of cold drinks to the counter. They stood back and admired their handiwork.

As Lydia started the kettle to boil, Clay and Harry arrived from the back door, and the others came from the main entry and filed into the kitchen. Willow accompanied Olivia and joined the other dogs. Clay walked over to give Ace and Maverick some attention. "How are you two?" He rubbed under both of their chins. "We left Hope and Chief at the house with Tyler. They're good watch dogs and can keep him company while we're here."

Heath pointed at the counter. "Lydia and I have dinner set and ready to cook but thought we could all hear from Harry before we eat."

Lydia poured some iced teas. "Please grab something to drink. Coffee's ready, and the water is hot for tea." She slipped the pasta into the oven to bake and set the timer to remind her to uncover it halfway through.

With a tilt of his head, Clay said, "We might as well use the great room. There are plenty of seats in there for all of us."

Heath made himself an Arnold Palmer and led the way down the hall to the great room, with the huge floor-to-ceiling fireplace. Harry and Clay followed, and she put a thick file on the hearth of the fireplace, and the two of them sat on the stone ledge, holding their iced teas. The dogs padded after them and sprawled across the floor between the conversation area in front of the fireplace and the large desk and table on the other side of the huge space, used when guests came to discuss ranch business.

Micki and Buck sat on one couch, and Olivia and Duke took the other, leaving the two leather chairs facing the fireplace for Heath and Lydia. Having spent most of her time in the kitchen and den, Lydia gazed around the huge room, imagining what it would be like at the holidays. She could picture a huge Christmas tree and a fire roaring.

Most of her Christmases in recent years had been spent in Gypsy. She always made something special and put up festive lights, but it wasn't the same as a family Christmas in a room like this one.

As she sipped her cup of hot tea, she couldn't take her eyes from the paintings of the horses. For one thing, they were huge, and the shiny horse depicted in them looked so lifelike. They demanded the adoration she gave them.

Harry took a long swallow from her glass and set it on a coaster. She reached for the file and set in on her lap. "The good news is, with it being an odd year, the legislature is in a long session and will be there until late June. Marcus is at the legislative building in Senator Robinson's office. We have eyes on him, and he hasn't left Salem since the article was published. He was there this weekend, working, going out for meals, and staying at his rental in Salem."

Harry looked across at Lydia. "I know that doesn't mean much since he could enlist someone to come here to harass you or hurt you, but at least we know where he is."

Lydia nodded and took another sip. All eyes were on Harry, waiting for more.

"That said, when Lydia told me about him, I figured we would find other victims like Lydia. I wanted to try to build a case against him based on collecting statements from others and show a habitual abuser. My old team talked to some trusted colleagues who've served at the Capitol, and they confirm lots of rumblings and rumors about Marcus. He likes to prey on young staffers. Sounds like there have been some complaints, but nothing ever happens, and the victims typically leave or move on. In some cases, they're given promotions or jobs, and their complaints are withdrawn. There is quite a bit of brushing things under rugs when it comes to politicians and their staffers. Their own ethics committees police such things, and nothing of substance ever comes from them."

Anger bubbled up inside Lydia. "That's exactly how Marcus operates. He believes money and power can buy whatever he needs or fix any mistake. He's a parasite."

Harry sighed. "I would agree." She looked back at her notes. "So, while it seems to be common knowledge among his colleagues and staffers, Marcus has managed to insulate himself and evade any real scrutiny. Your story about him also reminded me of a cold case from almost twenty years ago. An intern who was working at the legislature was murdered. At the time, it wasn't my case, but I followed it closely."

She had everyone's attention.

"A twenty-three-year-old woman, Claudia Vinton, a college student, was working as an intern for Senator Gregg Banks. She was seen leaving the building one night after work, and then she didn't show up the following morning. She was responsible and not known for partying, so when she didn't come to work, the office staff was worried and reported it to the Oregon State Police, who handle security at the Capitol. Initially, they dismissed it as typical intern behavior."

Lydia's throat went dry, and she took another sip from her cup.

"Claudia's body was found at Minto-Brown Park two days later. It's a huge park along the river. She'd been raped and strangled. She was wearing the same clothes she had worn the last time she was seen at work. She lived alone in a small studio near campus and the Capitol Building on Thirteenth Street."

The buzzer on the oven prompted Lydia to rise. Heath held out his hand. "I'll get it, just sit tight." He hurried to the kitchen, and Harry waited for him to return.

After Heath took his seat, Harry opened the file. "Claudia was an only child, and her parents lived in a small town in eastern Oregon. They were devastated and for years, would call to ask about the case. The forensics team retrieved DNA, but it didn't match anything in the system. In those days, the technology wasn't as good, and there weren't cameras on every corner or cell phone data to geofence and trace. The detectives did tons of interviews but came up empty. Claudia didn't socialize much and hadn't been seen with anyone. The people who lived in the main house and rented her the studio didn't keep track of her comings and goings. They hadn't seen anything."

Harry licked her lips. "The background Buck did on Marcus showed him working at the legislature at the time of Claudia's murder. Over his time working with various politicians, he's risen on the wealth ladder and since you knew him, Lydia, he's moved to an even swankier house. Along with Buck's background, my team reviewed Claudia's case. He'd been interviewed, as had everyone who was in the building the day of her disappearance. He was just starting out his career in politics. He worked on lots of campaigns while attending college in Portland and continued to do so after graduation. He ended up as a low-level staffer for then Representative Fuller, who went on to serve as a senator and then ran for US Senate, won, and went to DC."

Clay whistled. "When Lydia said connected, she wasn't

joking." Senator Fuller was still in DC, a fixture, as some would say. He serves on the powerful money committees.

Harry nodded. "Right. Marcus has been swimming in the political pond for decades, and he's surrounded by powerful friends. It does make me wonder why Senator Fuller didn't recruit Marcus to join him in DC. Perhaps he knew Marcus was a liability." She turned a few pages in the file. "I was hoping his DNA might be on file in the system, but it wasn't. He's never been convicted of a crime that would require the sample."

Harry glanced around the room. "Now, this next part is highly confidential, and I probably shouldn't share it, but I trust all of you and especially want Lydia to get a resolution so she can move on with her life and start living it."

Heath nodded and reached across for Lydia's hand. "I'll second that."

Everyone laughed, and some of the tension in the air evaporated. Harry made eye contact with Buck, Micki, Duke, and Olivia. "So, everybody understands this doesn't leave the room, right?"

All seven heads nodded at that same time.

"We..." she laughed. "I'm having a hard time not being all in on this one. I should say, *they*, my old team, put in a couple undercover officers in the janitorial staff at the legislature and this morning collected a water bottle and a paper coffee cup Marcus discarded in his office. They're at the lab and being examined now. The DNA collected from Marcus will be analyzed and compared to that from Claudia's case."

Harry closed the folder. "My gut feeling could be wrong, but this particular case was one that always haunted me when I'd see it come up on the unsolved list. Claudia's parents are some of the nicest people you'd ever meet. They'd fit right in here in Lavender Valley. Salt of the earth type. Claudia's dream was to become a lawyer, and they sacrificed to make that happen for her. Losing her broke them."

Duke slipped his arm around Olivia.

Harry rubbed the edge of the folder between her fingers. "Marcus was never on the radar for her murder. He was twenty-nine at the time and a virtual nobody. The detectives took hard looks at everyone in Claudia's life, concentrating on her classmates and circle at work. Ultimately, they surmised it must have been a random killing, but some of us were never convinced that was the case. Hearing Lydia talk about Marcus made me think he could be a viable suspect."

Tears slipped down Lydia's cheeks.

Olivia reached for a tissue from the box on the side table next to her. "Her poor parents. That's a long time to live without answers." She took another tissue and handed the box to Lydia.

"Far too long," said Harry, shaking her head. "They've asked the lab to rush the results, but we are at their mercy. It will be at least seventy-two hours before we can expect anything."

Harry took a long swallow from her glass. "We've got eyes on Marcus and will know if he leaves Salem, but like Lydia said before, he could hire someone to come here. We need to keep up with our security plan and keep Lydia confined to the ranch until we get those results and know where this is going."

Heath glanced over at Lydia and then met Harry's serious eyes. "What happens if the DNA matches?"

"They'll arrest the scumbag and charge him with murder. At that point, I suspect his circle of protection, power, and influence will diminish. Political animals, especially those facing another election, have a frail sense of loyalty when it comes to scandals. Once there's a chance of the stench of Marcus getting on them, he'll be on his own. At that point, there's a chance other women, like Lydia, will come forward to share their stories of abuse at his hands."

Clay shook his head. "The cockroaches always scurry in the sunlight."

Harry bit her bottom lip. "Those that may have helped sweep things under the rug will fear for their own reputations and could end up corroborating the accusations from other victims. It's hard to know."

"What's difficult," Buck said, "is the fact that the statute of limitations is long gone on most of these cases of abuse and assault. Not to say a pattern and history won't help, but to bring any type of actual case, it would require something current, say within the last year or two at most, unless it was a sexual assault. There are different statutes applicable to those crimes."

Harry nodded. "Right. I think it would be more of a chance for the victims to feel vindicated and have their accusations heard and taken seriously. It will also make the political power players squirm if they're caught up in covering up crimes of someone who turns out to be a murderer. A smart lawyer might decide to hold a press conference and bring it all out in the open."

Lydia dabbed her cheeks and balled up the tissue. "So, maybe by Friday, we'll have an answer? I hope he doesn't figure out he's a suspect."

Harry nodded. "Yes, we should know by Friday. We've kept the number of people at the legislature who know anything about this situation to two. Two people I know and trust. I'm confident they won't divulge anything. As I said, he's being watched around the clock, so try not to worry about him. Like you said, he may not take any action against you. I just don't want to take a chance that he contacts someone to help him, so I want to stay vigilant. At this point, we don't have enough to monitor his phone and frankly, if we went to a judge to get a warrant, we increase our chances of someone in the system tipping him off."

Micki's eyes widened. "This is like one of those mysteries we like to watch." She glanced over at Lydia. "That didn't come out right, sorry. I just meant it's exciting to know all these details behind the scenes."

Lydia smiled at her. "I know what you mean. I'm glad all of this might be over this week." She turned her eyes toward Harry. "Do you think he might have killed other women?"

She shrugged. "I think there's a strong possibility. They'll run his DNA against other cases, and we may get something that matches from there. If we do get a match with Claudia's case, things will start moving more quickly. We can secure warrants and examine his life with a fine-tooth comb."

Olivia turned toward Lydia. "I'm so glad you left and got away from Marcus. Your instincts were spot-on. Hearing this story about this young girl's murder sends shivers through me. I'm so glad you're here with us and not on your own."

Vera sprang from the floor and crawled up Lydia's legs and into her lap. All the fears and heartache Lydia was careful to hold deep inside burst forth. She couldn't stop the tears or the horrible sobs that sounded like a barking seal. Willow hurried to comfort Lydia and nestled next to her, leaning against her leg.

Heath left his chair and kneeled next to Lydia's. He rubbed the spot between her shoulder blades that always ached when she was tired or worked too hard. She closed her eyes and relished his touch. She hadn't felt such tenderness in a long time.

CHAPTER EIGHTEEN

Tuesday, Lydia woke late with Vera cuddled next to her in the huge bed. After a rough start last night, dinner was a huge success. Heath's kabobs were delicious, and everyone loved her penne pasta bake. Harry and Clay left early to take Tyler a plate and also took their dessert to go. Everyone else stayed late, visiting and enjoying cake on the patio.

As they were cleaning up the kitchen, Lydia noticed the leftover coffee and was about to dump it when it made her think of the chocolate cupcakes she loved, which used a bit of strong coffee in the batter. Heath insisted they stay up and make them. As soon as he bit into the tender chocolate cupcake with a rich ganache center and creamy chocolate frosting, he told her they were the best he'd ever eaten.

She didn't like to boast but had to agree.

After Harry explained the case to everyone last night, Lydia noticed how tired she looked. Her eyes were dark underneath, and she yawned a few times at dinner. Along with the drive back and forth to Salem, she'd worked on the case and had a meeting she had to attend this morning. It's no wonder she needed an early night. Lydia had to think of a way to repay her kindness.

As Lydia padded to the elegant bathroom, she grinned. Clay and Harry were the best. She thought of them as her own personal superheroes, who sprang into action whenever they sensed danger. She hoped they had some nice quiet time together last night.

Clay was sticking to the farm until this was over. He'd watch over Olivia, who needed to stay with the dogs. Heath would shadow Lydia, and she would confine herself to the ranch unless she was at the restaurant. Micki promised to come for a visit later in the day when she finished her work and gardening. With Harry working part of the day, she was the designated shopper and would fetch any supplies from town.

Freshly showered and dressed, Lydia found Heath sitting out on the patio off the kitchen. She poured herself some coffee, put some leftover cupcakes on a plate, and wandered out to join him.

"Morning," she said. "Anything new?"

"Not a thing. How are you this morning? Feeling better?" He eyed the cupcakes. "Breakfast of champions."

She smiled and took the chair next to his. "Much better, but I won't rest easy until we know about Marcus. I kept picturing that poor young girl and her parents. It makes me sick." She unwrapped a cupcake. "Chocolate makes everything better."

"I can't argue with that wisdom." He took one and bit into it. "I think you need a change of scenery," Heath said, with a slow grin. "Let's load up the dogs and take a picnic out to the edge of the ranch."

His words made her heart hum. "I love that idea. I'll put something together."

He held up his hand. "Already done. I've got the ice chest ready and in the back of the UTV."

"Wow, you're full of surprises."

He chuckled. "I actually thought about saddling up two horses, but I wasn't sure you'd be up for a horseback adventure."

Her eyes widened. "Gee, I've never ridden a horse, so you made the right call. I can't risk an injury right now. I need this job and with the festival coming up, we'll be busy. Maybe after things quiet down."

"I understand. Just think about it. We've got a couple of gentle ones that are perfect for people who don't ride or are a bit afraid of them."

She blushed. "Am I that transparent?"

That grin. The one that had the ability to lift her mood or in this case, make her weak in the knees, made her heart skip. "Just a little. I'll get the dogs loaded in the back, and you can hold Vera on your lap."

They finished their coffee and cupcakes, and she hurried to the guest room, where she retrieved her hat and sent Micki a text to let her know she'd be gone for a few hours.

Heath helped her get buckled in and made sure Vera was nestled in her lap before he got behind the wheel. As he drove, she relaxed against the back of the seat and took in the beauty of nature all around her.

The vivid green pastures were dotted with cattle, and they drove past two horses, glistening in the sun, on their way to the arena. The tops of the tall pine trees, so dark and noble, swayed in the slight breeze. The dark hills in the distance were a blunt contrast to the delicate blue sky. Bursts of color from a variety of wildflowers peppered the pathway and hills.

As they traveled the worn path past their pastures and outbuildings, Heath increased his speed, and the air swirled around her. She let the anxiety from last night float away with each wisp of wind.

By the time they reached the creek and parked in the shade of a large tree, she felt totally relaxed. The dogs stood, their tails wagging, and their eyes glued to Heath, waiting for his release command. He let them out, and they sprinted toward the water, wading into the creek. He took out the folding chairs he'd packed and set them up near the creek.

Heath returned to the UTV and set Vera on the ground, keeping hold of her leash with one hand and using the other to help Lydia up and out of the UTV. She glanced down at Vera, sniffing the air. "I don't quite trust her, since she's not used to all this open space."

"She'll probably follow Maverick and Ace, but we can keep her on her leash."

They wandered along the edge of the creek, and Vera put her paws in the water. The big dogs were out in the middle of it, splashing and playing. Lydia laughed. "We took the dogs out to the lake on Jewel's property. Everyone went swimming except for Vera. She seems to draw the line at the middle of her short legs."

"You never know, she might get used to it and become a water dog." He led the way to the chairs, and they sat, letting Vera have enough leash to get to the water.

"I only came out this far with Jewel a few times, but I can see why she loved it out here. Harry said Jewel wants her and Chuck's ashes interred out there under that big maple tree by the lake. We're planning a celebration of life to honor

Jewel. I want to do a big dinner in the lavender field after the festival."

"Count me in to help. Maybe I could be your sous chef?" He wiggled his eyebrows at her.

"That could be arranged." She sighed. "I'm not sure what to do about the menu. I want it to be special, but also reflect everything Jewel loved."

"Jewel never passed up the chance for a good old-fashioned barbecue. I'm sure you could work your magic around that."

"Maybe I could enlist you and Clay to be the grill masters?"

"Done," he said with a grin.

She gazed across the land. "It's so peaceful here. Makes you forget all your troubles." She chuckled. "Well, sort of. This whole thing with Marcus hanging over me is hard to shake."

"I know your first inclination was to run again, but I'm glad you stayed. One way or another, Marcus is going to be out of your life. Either he'll get arrested for murder, or he'll get a visit from me, and I'll make sure he understands to leave you alone."

His swagger and desire to help touched her deep in her soul. "I feel like such a fool and a weakling. I knew I'd never win against him, physically or mentally. It's tough to fight that much power and corruption."

"I get it. Especially on your own. At best, he's a bully, and it sounds like nobody has ever held him accountable. It makes you wonder what his parents must be like. My daddy made sure Clay and I knew harassing people, especially women, would bring about swift punishment."

She frowned. "I don't know anything about his family.

With Buck doing a background on him, I bet he does. We'll have to ask him."

Her cell phone chimed with a text and while she read it, he brought the ice chest over and removed two wrapped mini charcuterie boards and bottles of iced tea and lemonade.

She held the phone. "Cheryl said they've got a private party booked in for Thursday and need me to work. Are you okay with being my security that night? It won't be too late."

He nodded as he unwrapped the board. "Sure, whatever you need, I'm there."

She tapped in a reply. "When all this is over, I need to think of something special to repay you and everyone else. There's no way I could face all this on my own. If not for you and Clay and Harry, I'd already be miles away, looking for my next temporary job."

He took a swallow of tea and shook his head. "You don't owe anyone anything. Things don't work that way in Lavender Valley. People just pitch in and help and do whatever is needed. They don't expect a reward and don't keep track. They know the next time they need help, you'll be there for them."

He placed the board filled with all sorts of yummy cheese, fruit, and meat on the small pop-up table connected to the side of Lydia's chair. She opted for a bottle of iced tea and took a nibble of cheese while he unwrapped the other board. "I haven't had that sort of a connection to a community since I left here. Maybe a few from my class in culinary school. We were a tight-knit group."

He popped a few grapes in his mouth and ignored the pleading eyes of the dogs who'd hurried from the water as soon as the sound of plastic wrap opening reached them. "It's just one of the many things I love about living here. I've never lived anywhere else, so it's hard to compare, but I think we have something special here."

"You've never wanted to spread your wings and move somewhere bigger?"

He smirked and shook his head. "Nope. My roots are firmly planted on the ranch. Clay was gone for several years up in Lake Oswego. He had a contracting business and did really well, but when he came back, he came back for good."

"These last few years, I've been so focused on staying one step ahead of Marcus, I never dreamed of settling down anywhere. Now, though…"

Heath's blue eyes gazed at hers. "If I told you I think I'm starting to fall in love with you, would it make you want to stay?"

Her heart beat faster and faster. She was sure he could see it pounding in her neck. His sparkling eyes, his easy grin, his humor, and sincerity. It was all right there. He was the whole package, and he was falling in love with *her*. The men who had come in and out of her life were nothing like him. Lydia was convinced her skill in selecting men was permanently damaged. Until now.

"Are you sure that's not just the chocolate cupcakes talking?" She laughed.

He shook his head. "I felt that way even before I tasted your awesome cupcakes."

She reached across the space between their chairs, and he took her hand. "I think I feel the same way."

He leaned over closer to her and like a moth drawn to a flame, she met his lips with hers. She closed her eyes and swore she could see fireworks as his lips brushed over hers.

After a leisurely lunch and a bit of cuddling by the edge of the creek while the dogs dried in the warm sunshine, they loaded up and headed back to the ranch. As they pulled up to the back door, Micki texted to let Lydia know she was on her way.

She left Heath to unload the UTV and hurried inside with Vera. She took a bag of the chocolate chip cookies she'd made for Heath out of the freezer and left them to thaw. After washing her hands and running a brush through her hair before resecuring it back in its ponytail, she brewed a fresh pitcher of iced tea.

Minutes later, the front doorbell rang out and with Vera at her heels, Lydia opened the door to welcome Micki. "Heath's out back putting the UTV away. We took a picnic down to the creek."

"Oh, that sounds wonderful. It's a gorgeous day." She followed Lydia to the kitchen.

"I've got some fresh iced tea. Just brewed, so we'll need to add lots of ice." She pointed outside. "We could sit on the patio." Vera wandered over to her bed and settled into it.

"That would be lovely. I meant to tell you last night but with all the revelations from Harry, it slipped my mind. Since it was our normal Monday family dinner, I called Georgia to let her know we wouldn't be able to video chat. I just said you were dealing with some serious issues and gave her an abbreviated overview. Of course, I didn't know what Harry told us last night."

"I know this whole thing has disrupted our routine." Lydia shook her head as she loaded three glasses with ice and added some to the pitcher.

"Well, that's not your doing. Georgia wanted you to know she was thinking of you and would add you to her nightly prayers."

Lydia brought her hand to her chest. "What a sweetheart. I really hope I can put all this behind me in the next few days." She added the cookies and a few cupcakes to a plate and carried it to the patio.

Heath joined them and let the dogs wander on the grass below the patio. "Hey, Micki." He pointed at the cupcakes and cookies. "I guarantee whatever your troubles, one of those will fix it."

She laughed. "It can't hurt to try." She took a cupcake and bit into it. "Wow, I think you're right."

Lydia met her eyes. "So, tell me all about your visit with your sister. Was she faking, as you suspected?"

Micki's smile slipped from her face. "Yes. After I confronted her and tripped her up a time or two, bringing up some childhood memories, she finally came clean." She shook her head. "Bottom line she's a habitual liar and beyond irresponsible. I think she thought it would be easier to keep playing along with the whole amnesia thing, which was real in the beginning. She doesn't want to face reality at this point."

Lydia took a cookie from the plate. "Does she know she'll be arrested when she's released?"

"I didn't bring it up, but I know the police have been there to see her, and I'm sure they explained it. Buck thinks she may get off with minimal jail time, maybe even probation or community service. He said her being hurt and possibly in need of therapy and medical care will play into the sentence. She'll probably lose her license for up to a year. She doesn't have a car, so not sure that matters. Part of me hoped she'd be in jail for several months, just so I didn't have to deal with her." She sighed. "I know that makes me a horrible person."

Lydia patted Micki's arm. "No, it just makes you human."

"I did suggest she get serious and work with the social worker to apply for housing. I spoke with the social worker privately and let her know we'd been estranged for years, and I had no interest in fostering a relationship with her. I think they just presumed I would be taking her in and helping. I know how disappointed Meg will be with me, but I just can't do it."

Heath poured more tea into his glass. "Sounds like she hasn't exactly given you a reason to trust her."

"I was pretty tough on her today," said Micki. "I made it clear she's going to have to not only work hard on her therapy to regain her health, but she's going to have to face the music when it comes to the criminal charges, commit to staying clean, find a job, and secure a place to live. I also threw in that she needed to pay me back the five grand she extorted."

"That's a big to-do list," said Lydia.

Micki sighed. "I honestly don't wish anything bad to happen to her. I hope she uses this as an opportunity to clean up her life, and I don't expect her to ever pay me back, but I'm not up for welcoming her into my life like nothing ever happened." Tears filled Micki's eyes. "She's inflicted a lot of pain and damage, and it's going to take time before I can even think of forgiving her. If ever."

Heath slid the plate of cupcakes closer to her. "I think you need another one."

CHAPTER NINETEEN

Wednesday and Thursday, Lydia did her best to keep busy. Each time she sat, her thoughts went to Marcus and the DNA tests. The waiting was grueling, and she was on a constant prowl for distractions.

Over too many cups of coffee, she and Heath commiserated about Micki's situation with her sister. Micki seemed better after they visited Tuesday night, but the future weighed on her. Lydia assured her she and all the others would be there to help her through whatever came.

With Harry home and off work for a few days, Clay returned to the ranch and took care of a few things, while Heath kept watch over Lydia. They filled their days with television, lots of walks with the dogs, and Lydia made several batches of dog cookies and human treats.

The dogs were happy to be her taste testers and loved the strawberry yogurt frozen treats she made for them. They sat outside and stayed busy licking them.

Heath kept her company while she baked. He shared some stories about growing up in Lavender Valley and how his grandparents were the ones who started the ranch, but his dad made it into a success. He reminisced about his grandparents growing peaches and strawberries and summers spent churning homemade ice cream.

It sounded heavenly, and a tiny part of Lydia was envious of the life Heath had enjoyed. Growing up here, surrounded by a loving family, shaped him into the man he was today. Luckily, Jewel had saved Lydia and given her five years of happiness and hope, or her future would have been nonexistent. Part of Lydia always wanted a big family of her own. Maybe that wish was finally coming true.

By the time Thursday afternoon arrived, Lydia was more than ready to get out of the house and work. Even though they left from the ranch, Heath made her lie down in the backseat of his truck so anyone watching the road wouldn't see her.

He parked his truck in the back with the other employees and walked by her side as they made their way through the fenced backyard and to the rear entrance into the kitchen. He left her at the door and said, "I'm just going to check around the perimeter, and I'll meet you inside."

By the time Heath made it to the front entrance, Lydia was standing next to Cheryl at the hostess station. A couple of regulars were seated at the bar, and Cheryl was on the phone booking a reservation. As soon as she disconnected, Cheryl put her pen down and smiled at both of them.

Heath tipped his hat. "Any unusual diners or inquiries about Lydia?"

She shook her head. "Nothing. We're starting to get summer tourists in, so a few strange faces, but not a word about Lydia."

He nodded and found a seat in the lounge that gave him a view of the entrance. The bartender brought him an iced tea, and he settled in for the duration. Lydia promised to bring him a snack later and left him to people watch.

Cyrus put Lydia in charge of the food for the private party. A longtime customer was celebrating her seventy-fifth birthday with friends. They had specifically requested Lydia's mushroom risotto and roasted chicken. As Lydia mixed the herbs with butter and lemon zest and a bit of honey, she relaxed. She focused on the food and left her worries behind, back in her happy place.

With the chickens in the oven, she tackled the brussels sprouts and carrots, seasoning the already sliced veggies and adding them to a baking sheet to roast. Her secret was a drizzle of high-quality maple syrup when they had about five more minutes to roast.

She could make the mushroom risotto in her sleep and by the time the chickens were done, she had it finished and ready and pulled out the veggies, looking perfectly caramelized.

She plated up the meals, and the servers were off to deliver them. She was entitled to a free meal and opted to make another plate with the special birthday dinner selections and asked Cheryl to deliver it to Heath. She had plenty of leftovers to eat at home and hated the thought of Heath hungry as he waited for her.

The birthday partygoers brought in a special cake from the Sugar Shack, so dessert was handled except for delivering it to the table, and the servers helped with slicing it. Her work was done, but Lydia pitched in and helped Cyrus get caught up on the dishes in the queue. Thursdays were typically quiet, but with the summer season, business was already booming.

As she was about to call it a day, Cheryl came into the kitchen. "The birthday girl, Eloise, has requested you come to say hello. They loved your food, and she wants to thank you. Can you spare a few minutes?"

Lydia untied the strings of her stained apron and checked to make sure her uniform was clean. "Sure, I'll stop by, then I'm going to clock out."

She made her way through the lounge and past Heath who was seated in the small room where they'd eaten dinner when they came. The party was in the room on the other side of the fireplace, where she could already hear their laughter.

She ducked in and spotted the birthday girl, wearing a glittery crown and a boa, at the head of the table. Lydia looked down at the woman, with beautiful white hair and kind eyes, decked out in a pink pantsuit that matched the boa. "Hi Eloise, Cheryl said you wanted to see me. I'm Lydia."

Eloise reached out her hands. "Oh, wonderful. Thank you for taking the time to come. We just wanted to tell you how absolutely wonderful your meal was. It was perfection."

All the people around the table, a mixture of single women and a few couples, nodded and added their praise. Lydia glanced over and murmured her thanks to them. She turned her attention back to Eloise. "I hope you have a wonderful birthday, and I'm so happy you enjoyed the meal."

"I could eat your risotto for every meal." She laughed and squeezed Lydia's hand. "Thanks again, dear."

Lydia waved and left them to visit and enjoy the dessert coming soon. Basking in their kind compliments, which never got old, Lydia was still smiling as she came from the room and around the corner to the fireplace. A woman with long, gray hair walked toward her.

Lydia moved closer to the fireplace and the small table with a display of their wines to let her pass by. She assumed she was joining the birthday gathering. Instead of moving away from Lydia, the woman stepped closer.

That's when Lydia saw the glint of a knife in the woman's hand. Her arm rose, and she screamed, "This is for Marcus, you bitch."

Lydia pivoted to the side and grabbed two bottles of wine from the table. As the woman lunged at her with the knife, Lydia swung the bottle out and met her arm, connecting with a solid blow. The knife fell to the ground.

The woman kept coming, her eyes crazed and her mouth open. Without hesitating, Lydia swung the second bottle, a bit like a backhand tennis move, and shattered it against the woman's head.

Heath was at her side before the woman hit the ground. Lydia's heart was racing, and she stared at the floor. The woman's gray hair had slipped off her head, revealing a mass of dark hair underneath it. The wig rested in a puddle of dark red wine, surrounded by shards of green glass.

Lydia couldn't stop staring at the woman.

Heath's strong arms held her and led her away from the attacker.

CHAPTER TWENTY

Heath ushered Lydia through the lounge and toward the kitchen. They passed by Cheryl who was trying to keep the customers calm. She caught Heath's eye and whispered, "The police are on the way, and I requested an ambulance."

Heath only nodded and kept pushing Lydia forward and through the door to the kitchen. Cyrus looked up from his station and frowned. "Is everything okay?"

Lydia shook her head and let Heath lead her to the small employee lounge, where he pulled out a chair for her. Moments later, one of the servers brought her a glass of water.

With her hands shaking, she reached out for it and took a long swallow. "Do you think that woman's okay?" The sound of sirens came from the street.

Heath shook his head. "Don't know. Don't care. You're the only one I'm worried about." He took her hands in his. "Are you hurt anywhere? Did she cut you?"

"No, I hit her with the bottle before she got me."

"Do you recognize her?"

With a shake of her head, Lydia sighed. "No, I don't think so. She was wearing a wig, so I'm not sure." Her shoulders slumped. "I thought she was going to the birthday party."

"Yeah, she wasn't on my radar at all. I assumed the same."

Between sips of water, Lydia took deep breaths, forcing her heart to calm. Minutes later, Harry came through the back door of the kitchen and into the small room where Lydia sat. She knelt next to Lydia. "How are you doing?"

"I'm okay. Do you know who that woman is?"

Harry shook her head. "Not yet. I just wanted to check on you. Chief Phillips will take your statement, then Heath can get you home. As soon as we know more, I'll be in touch." She placed a hand on Lydia's shoulder.

As she stood, she caught Heath's eye. "Clay's staying at the farm. We don't want to let our guard down until we know more. I'll give you a call later."

Minutes later, an older man in uniform came through the door and introduced himself as Chief Phillips. He asked Heath to wait outside the room and then asked Lydia to tell him what happened. Then he had her write a statement. As he slipped it into a folder, he met Lydia's eyes. "I'm glad you weren't hurt. We've got lots of people to interview and several statements to collect from those who saw the incident. We aren't sure of the woman's connection to Marcus, but with her screaming his name, it's obvious there is one. I'll let you know as soon as we know anything, but it will probably be tomorrow. Try to get some rest tonight."

He called out for Heath and asked him to step outside so he could interview him. A few minutes later, Heath came through the door. "Chief Phillips says we can go now."

Heath carried Lydia's handbag and kept hold of her hand as they left the kitchen. They reached the door, and Cyrus hurried to her side. "If you're not up to working tomorrow, don't worry about it. Just take care of yourself."

Suddenly exhausted and shakier, Lydia nodded. "I'll let you know."

Heath bundled her into the passenger seat and retrieved a blanket he used for the dogs from the backseat. He put it around her before getting behind the wheel.

The hum of the radio lulled her to sleep, and she woke with a start when Heath opened his door. After getting her in the house, he led her down the hallway to her guest room.

She fell onto the bed, and the last thing she remembered was Heath tugging off her shoes and Vera's tongue on her cheek.

Friday morning, the aroma of fresh brewed coffee tickled her nose. Her eyes fluttered at the filtered sunlight coming through the window. Vera's head rested on the pillow next to hers.

As her eyes blinked to focus, she saw Heath, his hair wet from a shower, sitting on the rolled arm upholstered bench at the end of the bed. "Hey," he said. "I didn't want to startle you. I brought you in some coffee." He pointed at the steaming cup on her nightstand. "It's almost noon."

She sat up, noting she still wore her uniform, and reached for the cup. She took her first sip and closed her eyes. When she opened them, she noticed the stack of pillows and blankets on the chair next to the door that led out to her patio. "Did you sleep in here last night?"

"Yeah, I slept in the chair and on this couch thing. I didn't want you to be alone after last night."

Her heart swelled. He was the real deal. "That was sweet of you, thanks."

He rose and collected the linens. "Well, I'll leave you to it. Clay's coming over and said he's bringing donuts from the Sugar Shack. Vera already ate her breakfast with the other dogs. I just brought her back in with the coffee delivery."

"Thanks for taking good care of her." At the mention of pastries, Lydia's stomach reminded her she hadn't eaten last night. "The Sugar Shack sounds perfect. I'll be quick."

She took another gulp of coffee before darting under the stream of warm water. As she let it work its way into her tight muscles, she flashed back to the crazy look in that woman's eyes as she lunged at her. She was thankful for the wine display, since without those heavy bottles, she wouldn't have had any type of defensive weapon. Heath was at her side quickly, but she feared the woman would have stabbed her before he could get there.

Despite the warmth of the shower, she shuddered. More than anything, she wanted all of this to be over. She couldn't wait to hear from Harry or Chief Phillips. The more she thought about going back to work tonight, the more anxious she became. She needed some space.

After getting dressed and toweling her hair, leaving it to dry naturally, she sent a text to Cyrus and Cheryl and let them know she wouldn't be in tonight. She promised to update them as soon as she could.

Vera was waiting patiently at the foot of the bed and after making it, Lydia picked her up and cuddled her close under her chin. "You're the best girl, aren't you?"

She collected her coffee cup, and they made their way down the long hallway to the kitchen. Heath and Clay were both sitting at the counter, the dogs at their feet.

"Morning, Clay," said Lydia, refilling her cup.

"How are you doing?" he asked.

"Okay, just anxious. I decided to take tonight off. I'm uneasy going back there until I know more."

Clay nodded. "Totally understand that. Harry just got home about an hour ago and needs to sleep, but she expects to have more details later this afternoon. I told her I'd come check on you, but I need to get back so she can rest easy." He climbed off the chair and rinsed his empty cup at the sink. "I'm glad you're okay, Lydia. That was quick thinking on your part last night."

Heath shook his head. "Sure was. I was watching everyone in the restaurant, and the lady slipped right by me. I never gave her a second look. She looked harmless."

"I never expected Marcus to engage a woman to come after me. I just assumed it would be a man, so I was caught off guard too. I'm just dying to know who she is."

Clay gave Maverick a few more pets before saying goodbye. He put a hand on Lydia's shoulder as he walked by her. "Harry will call as soon as she can. I know lots of people are involved, trying to get answers."

"Thanks, Clay. I'll be right here waiting."

She settled into the chair Clay vacated and plucked a cinnamon roll from the box. She gestured to the other pastries and donuts. "Do you want one?"

"Already had two while we were waiting for you." He grinned. "They're good, but I think your cupcakes are better."

She smiled and laughed. "That's high praise."

Heath pointed at his cell phone. "I've already taken a couple of calls from Curt at the newspaper. He wanted to know what happened at the restaurant last night and if I saw anything. I, of course, declined to comment as did Cheryl and Cyrus."

"Oh, man, just what I need. More publicity. So much for

all the years I spent living under the radar."

"I told Curt his best bet was to talk to the police, and I'd pass along his desire to interview you, but that I knew you wouldn't be saying anything until the investigation was complete."

She nodded and put her fork down. "I'm going to scramble some eggs. I need something to balance out the sugar. Do you want some?"

"Sure, sounds good."

In no time, she whisked eggs together, added in some shredded cheese, and slid them out of the pan and onto two plates.

After they ate and cleaned up the kitchen, Heath suggested they take the dogs for a walk to kill some time.

He led them around the back of the house and to the huge barn. Vera was sniffing at every new scent, holding up their progress. They finally reached the entrance, and Lydia's eyes widened. The barn and all the outbuildings matched the architecture and style of the main house.

She picked up Vera and held her as they meandered down the large center aisle made with pavers. Heath pointed out the stalls where the horses stood. The aroma of hay and grass and leather permeated the air.

She stopped in front of a shiny chestnut horse with gentle eyes. Heath reached up and petted the horse. "This is Merlot. You've got good instincts. She's a mellow, gentle horse. The one I'd probably pick for you to ride."

Lydia marveled at the stature of Merlot. "She's gorgeous."

"My dad had a gift when it came to picking horses, breeding them, raising them. He left a real legacy."

"The ranch is spectacular. I would have loved to have met him and your mom. They definitely sound special and raised two wonderful sons."

Sadness filled his eyes. "I miss them both so much. Memories of them are everywhere. Etched into the very soil. I think that's part of why I can't imagine living anywhere else. I feel close to them here."

"I get that. Being at Jewel's house is more emotional than I imagined. Sometimes, I find myself expecting her to come through the door. I miss her smile, and her hugs were the best."

"I would agree. She really stepped up when our mom passed away. She seemed to have an infinite capacity to give to those in need of her love. She'll always have a special place in my heart."

"She saved me once, and it looks like her idea to reunite us all here at the farm might just save me again."

"We always say she had a knack for knowing what we needed before we even knew it. Her timing was uncanny that way."

He took Vera from her and urged Lydia to let Merlot smell her hand and pet her snout. She giggled as the horse's lips brushed across her hand. "Tickles a little."

"She's a sweetheart. Go ahead and pet her."

Lydia ran her hand over her silky snout, and Merlot pushed against it. She flicked her ears, and Lydia kept rubbing her, reaching further up her head as Merlot lowered it. "See," said Heath, "you're already fast friends."

As she kept her hand on Merlot, Lydia glanced around. The wood gleamed, and the floor was cleaner than most sidewalks. "This barn is beautiful and pristine. I never imagined a barn that smelled good."

He laughed. "Our dad was obsessed with keeping a clean barn and grounds. He entertained lots of prospective buyers and investors and liked everything looking its best. Even without anyone visiting, he expected things to be shipshape. Clay and I inherited that same pickiness."

"There are worse things. I was raised in actual filth most of the time. My mother didn't have that same affliction as your dad. I tried to keep my room clean; the rest of the house was a lost cause."

He reached for her hand and squeezed it. "You're nothing like your mother, Lydia. I'm beyond sorry for all that happened to you, but you've risen far above it all. You're talented, successful, and a clean freak. I can tell by watching you in the kitchen and the care you take with everything."

She sighed and smiled at him. "I definitely inherited her ability to pick the wrong men. If I hadn't met Marcus, I wouldn't be in this mess now."

He raised his brows. "If you hadn't met Marcus, maybe you wouldn't be here right now. Trust me, I've played the game of beating myself up about the past. Bad decisions, poor choices, stupid stuff, not appreciating my parents enough when they were here. It's usually nonproductive. It's lessons we've all learned, sometimes the hard way. What counts is what you do moving forward."

His simple words had a profound impact. It also made her realize the men she'd spent her time with never talked to her about anything important. She'd had more meaningful conversations with Heath in the last few weeks than she'd ever had with Marcus.

Heath was a man who didn't profess to be perfect. He didn't dwell on his flaws or the past. He embraced the present and did his best to make the future better.

She nodded at him. "You're right. I want a better future and maybe if I'm not obsessed with running all the time, I can have one."

Maybe she was looking right at it.

CHAPTER TWENTY-ONE

Heath's phone chimed, and he pulled it from his pocket. "Clay says Harry's in town at the police department. She should have more information and will be able to give you an update on the case around five tonight and if you're up for it, Buck offered to pick up pizzas, and everyone can gather here at the ranch."

"Yes, yes. For sure." She took Vera from him so he could text a reply.

He finished his text and slipped the phone back in his pocket. "All set." He slipped an arm around her shoulder. "It's going to be okay. It'll all be over soon."

They left Merlot and walked back outside, making their way toward the house. When they reached the edge of the grass, Lydia bent down and let Vera free to join Maverick and Ace as they romped toward the back of the house.

Worry etched her face as she glanced over at Heath. He gripped her hand. "I told you I'd be there for you, no matter what. I promise I will be. We'll get through all this."

She took in a deep breath of the fresh summer air. No

matter what happens, being here, surrounded by people who cared about her, was better than being on her own, running and hoping she could find a good place to stay for a few months before she'd get scared again and leave.

They shooed the dogs inside and then headed out to the shady end of the patio to lounge on the cool concrete and stone. Vera stretched out between her two big friends brought a smile to Lydia's face.

She put her hands on her hips and eyed the oven. "I think I'll make some brownies while we wait."

He turned on some music and as he poured them both some iced tea, he chuckled. "I think I've gained five pounds since you've been here stress-baking. I'm going to have to join a gym if this keeps up."

She laughed as she gathered the ingredients. "I can't picture you at a gym. Does Lavender Valley even have a gym?"

"We had one of those 24-hour places open up in an old strip mall, but it didn't last. Most of us get plenty of exercise taking care of our land and animals. Plus, you've got acres to walk or run if you want. Personally, I don't run unless something big and scary is chasing me."

She laughed and stirred chocolate chips into the batter before pouring it into a pan. She added more flour and ingredients into the bowl. As she stirred, she looked over at Heath. "Do you have any bourbon?"

He chuckled. "My dad was a big fan. I forgot to tell you. That statue out front and those huge paintings. That's Whiskey Grin, his prized racehorse. He always had a horse named Whiskey. Most of his horses were named after liquor, and Mom liked wine, so she got to name a few."

"Merlot," she whispered.

He smiled and retrieved a bottle of bourbon from the cabinet. "Here you go."

She added a couple of tablespoons to the batter, along with pecans. "These are bourbon pecan and delicious."

He bent closer to the bowl. "Smells great."

She finished adding chocolate chips and scooped the batter into another pan. She slid both into the oven and went about washing the dishes. As she washed the bowl, he took a towel from a drawer. "You know we have a dishwasher, right?"

She chuckled. "I'm on autopilot. I'm so used to washing dishes by hand in the motorhome, I never think about a dishwasher."

He took the bowl from her and held her hand in his.

His touch and the affection in his eyes made hers sting with tears. He didn't say a word, just set the bowl on the counter and wrapped his arms around her.

She tried but failed to contain the tears that wouldn't stop flowing. As she sobbed, he tightened his hold on her. He smelled like the barn, mixed with something citrusy. As she calmed and caught her breath, she savored the feeling of being in his arms.

Protected.

Safe.

Loved.

All the things she'd been searching for, and they were here the whole time, right next door to Jewel.

They stayed that way, swaying to the tune of "I Need You" as the scent of baking brownies wafted around them. As the song ended, she whispered in his ear, "I need you."

He moved his head and found her eyes, grinning as he covered her lips with his.

A few minutes before five o'clock, Lydia paced the kitchen. They had the dogs fed, plates and utensils out on the counter, iced tea, lemonade, beer, and wine at the ready, and brownies baked and cut.

She couldn't shake the anxiety creeping over her. She never thought this day would come when she might be rid of Marcus. He was so slippery, she wasn't convinced he'd ever be held to account. She hoped Clay was right, and Harry would nail him.

As she worried, the dogs darted to the door. Clay came through it, herding Chief, Hope, and Willow into the house. He held the door for Harry, Olivia, and Duke, followed by Micki and Buck, holding boxes from Brick's.

Heath took the boxes out of Micki's hands and led them all into the kitchen.

Lydia turned the oven on low and opened it so Heath could slide the boxes onto the racks. "I can't eat a thing until I know what's going on."

Harry smiled. "I've got good news. We can sit, and I'll tell you all about it."

Heath and Clay filled glasses and got everyone settled on the patio. Heath poured Lydia a glass of wine and a tall ginger ale and placed them both in front of her before he took the chair next to hers.

Harry had her file folder with her and flipped it open. "The DNA from Claudia's case matched Marcus."

Olivia gasped, and Lydia's stomach flipped.

Harry continued, "Marcus was arrested two hours ago and is being held in Salem. He's undergoing questioning and will go before a judge on Monday. They timed it that way on purpose, so he'd spend the weekend in jail."

Lydia swallowed hard and took a gulp from her ginger ale. "I hope he's not granted bail."

Harry jaw tightened. "It's up to a judge, but the prosecutor will argue that he's a flight risk and a danger to the community."

She looked at her notes. "They also have a preliminary match on at least one old case. It's a sexual assault from five years ago. They'll have to do a bit more analysis and review the case, but that's another mark against him. At minimum, he'll be charged with murder, solicitation for murder, and conspiracy."

"What a degenerate piece of crap," said Heath, shaking his head.

Harry arched her brows. "It gets better." She looked across the table at Lydia. "The woman who attacked you at the restaurant is connected. Her name is Deidre Hartwing. She was taken in as a foster child by Marcus' parents."

Everyone around the table went wide eyed at the startling revelation.

Harry consulted the file. "She's three years younger than Marcus and attended the same college as Claudia. She's being held in Jackson County at the detention center in Medford for assaulting Lydia."

She reached for a sip from her Arnold Palmer. "Marcus' father died several years ago, and his mother has dementia. She's cared for by a home nurse and various staff. The father was a wealthy, prominent banker, which is how Marcus got his start in politics."

Lydia held up her hand. "So, Marcus had Deidre come here to attack me?"

Harry grimaced. "It's murkier than that, but in essence, yes. Deidre was very troubled as a young girl. She has scars all over her arms from cutting herself and has a hard time with impulse control, anxiety, and anger. I believe Marcus used her as a tool. She's the perfect patsy, in a sense. Mentally unstable, easily manipulated, and totally infatuated with him. So, he didn't have to pay her, just direct her."

Harry glanced down at her notes. "He told Deidre you were a threat to him and treated him poorly, lied about him, and he was worried you would ruin his life. She thought shooting you would be best, but he told her a gun would be problematic and that she should use a knife. He suggested the disguise and told her to run away after she stabbed you."

Micki's eyes widened. "Wow. Did she just get to Lavender Valley yesterday or has she been here longer?"

"She rented a car and drove from Portland on Thursday. Unfortunately, as Lydia suspected, the newspaper article led Marcus and Deidre right to her."

Heath shook his head. "This guy gets more disgusting by the minute."

Harry bobbed her head. "Lydia was right when she pegged him as a narcissistic psychopath. I suspect he engaged in an inappropriate relationship with Deidre at a young age. Her loyalty and infatuation with him is the kind of stuff they put in movies."

Lydia's shoulder slumped, and she took a drink from her wine glass. "So, you said Deidre went to college with Claudia. Do you think she was involved in her murder?"

"From what we can tell, Deidre most likely lured Claudia to a location where Marcus raped and killed her. I can't say for certain that she was present or involved, but from what we know at this point, she was an accomplice."

Heath reached for Lydia's hand and laced his fingers through hers. Lydia sighed. "That is disgusting and vile."

Harry nodded. "Everyone agrees. Marcus is demented and while Deidre is responsible for attacking you, in reality, she was the weapon Marcus used. I honestly don't know that she could pass a psych evaluation. Sometimes people try to pretend they're mentally unfit to escape responsibility, but everyone agrees, she's the real deal. She needs to be in a mental hospital."

Duke drummed his fingers against his glass of lemonade. "It makes you wonder what the parents knew and why they didn't get her help."

Harry's eyes narrowed. "Exactly. The one good thing that might come from all this is that Deidre will get the help she should have gotten years ago. Not sure how much good it will do now, and her future is grim."

Olivia leaned against Duke. "Did someone tell Claudia's parents?"

Harry's face softened. "Salem sent detectives to tell them in person. They didn't want them to hear about it on the news, so they set out before they actually arrested him and let them know right when it happened. They're elderly and not in the best of health, but they were relieved to know Claudia's killer had been captured. This case is so sad."

Micki and Olivia both wiped their eyes.

After a healthy swallow of ginger ale, Lydia turned toward Harry. "Is there any chance he'll get out of this? Get away with it?"

Harry frowned. "I don't think so. The case is rock solid. DNA is hard to fight and if the rape case is confirmed, that's another strike. They're still running open cases, so more things could pop up. From what the investigators told me, he started off with bravado, denying everything, demanding he speak with Senator Robinson and that he'd send a lawyer who would have him out in minutes."

She grinned and added, "Let's just say his confidence faded as they revealed what they knew and some of the more damning evidence. They're going through his phone, social media, computers, all of it. Not to mention, swarming the legislature to interview everyone who ever shook his hand."

After another sip from her glass, she turned toward Lydia. "On that note, they want to interview you and get as much information about Marcus' circle of friends and colleagues, in addition to your written statement related to the abuse you suffered and his threats."

Lydia nodded and sat up straighter. "No problem. I'll do whatever it takes." She glanced across the table at Buck. "Marcus never mentioned any siblings, did he have any?"

He shook his head. "No, no siblings, and his parents were both only children, so no extended family. From what I can tell, his mother has been supporting the foster daughter. I can't find any employment history on Deidre at all."

Harry closed the folder. "I did hear from my old boss. Sounds like Senator Fuller and Senator Robinson are both distancing themselves from Marcus already. I think when more layers of this onion get peeled, they will feed whatever carcass of Marcus is left to the wolves."

Lydia swallowed a sip of wine. Her stomach had calmed. "So, it sounds like I'm safe now. He and Deidre are both in custody."

Harry nodded. "Yes, I think she's heading to a psych ward, and the prosecutor is feeling strong about the argument to deny Marcus bail."

"Maybe life can get back to normal for all of us. I really can't thank you all enough for helping and your willingness to upset your routines for me. I really appreciate it." She glanced over at Heath. "I've been trying to think of a way to repay you all and haven't come up with anything worthy. Heath tells me it's just how things work in Lavender Valley. So, please know if you ever need my help, you've got it."

Her voice began to crack. "How about those pizzas?"

After pizza and brownies, everyone said their goodbyes. They left Lydia with hugs and warm thoughts. Clay walked Harry outside and when he came back in, he announced that he was off to bed for some much-needed sleep. He and Maverick padded down the hallway to his wing.

Heath gathered the open wine bottles and refilled Lydia's glass with red wine. The sun was edging toward the horizon and made for a gorgeous backdrop of pink and orange. Candles flickered on the table, and Lydia stared at the flame reflected in her wine glass.

He took another of the bourbon pecan brownies. "I think these are the best brownies I've ever had."

She smiled. "Everyone seemed to like them." She took a sip from her glass. "Mmm, that's a good one."

"One of my mom's favorites." He reached for his bottle of beer. "It's not going to be the same around here when you go back to the farm. I've gotten used to having you around."

"I appreciate you babysitting me, but I'm sure you'll be glad to get back to your normal life." She sighed. "I'm trying to figure out what my normal life will be. Part of me doesn't want to go back to the restaurant and be reminded of Deidre and Marcus."

"I'm sure Cyrus and Cheryl would understand if you decided it was too much. You could probably use some time to distance yourself from all of it."

"I don't want to leave them in a lurch, but I think you might be right. I liked working there and being back in a real kitchen, but the idea of going back there freaks me out right now."

"The Riverside Grille and the Back Door Bistro are both great restaurants, and I'm sure they'd be happy to have you, especially for the summer. I'm happy to introduce you."

She reached for his hand. "You are so kind to me. I appreciate the offer. I definitely need a job but was talking to Micki tonight about the festival. I'm beginning to think I might need to dial back any ideas I have about work and pour that energy into all the things I want to make to support the farm. Right now, I don't need the money."

"That sounds like a good idea. The festival will be fun, and you'll get to spend more time with everyone."

"I was thinking about that this morning. Jewel wanted us all to come to the farm because she thought we'd be good for each other. Be a family. So far, that's proven to be true. I've spent so many years worrying about Marcus and running, I've never really thought about what I want long term. I was focused on survival."

He put his other hand on to one of hers. "You're in the perfect place to rest and recover. You're safe now."

They held hands, sipped drinks, and ate brownies until thousands of shimmering stars covered the dark sky above them. Lydia leaned back and stared up at the sky and sighed. She loved it here and for the first time in years, she realized she didn't have to leave.

CHAPTER TWENTY-TWO

S aturday morning, Lydia stretched across the huge bed and looked at Vera. "We need to pack up and go home today, little one."

She booted the dog off the bed and stripped the sheets, leaving them in a pile by the door. After her shower, she packed up her toiletries and added the towels she used to the pile of laundry.

She stared at her phone and sat on the bench at the end of the bed, hitting the button to dial Cheryl. After she talked about it last night, she realized each time she thought about returning to the restaurant, anxiety flooded through her. Heath was right. She needed time to rest and recover not just from the attack, but from years of running and having fear dominate her every move.

Cheryl was more than understanding and told her if she decided she wanted to come back, there would always be a place for her in their kitchen. She assured Lydia they understood and even expected it.

With that chore out of the way, her shoulders relaxed.

She felt better already. After packing up her tote bag and checking once more to make sure she collected everything, she toted the pile of linens in her arms and led Vera down the hall to the kitchen.

Heath was pouring a cup of coffee and hurried to help her with the laundry. "You didn't need to do that."

"Yes, I do. I'll get the sheets started in the washer and can put a new set on if you point me to them."

He shook his head. "Just sit. Clara comes on Tuesday and will get everything shipshape. She doesn't like it when we clean before she comes. She loves taking care of things and feeling useful."

He marched the pile into the laundry room and returned a few minutes later with a tiny bowl filled with Vera's breakfast. "Clay already took the dogs and headed out."

Vera dug into her meal, and Lydia smiled and took the cup he offered. "I could tell he was happy to be home and in his own bed. He's had a week of very little sleep. Poor guy."

"He'll be fine. I'm glad you stayed last night."

"Well, I couldn't tear myself away from the sunset and then that blanket of stars. Everything seems more beautiful, more intense out here. And, after all that wine, I was too tired to even think about the short ride back to the farm."

She cradled the cup in her hands. "I called Cheryl and told her I wasn't coming back."

His eyes widened. "Good for you. I think it's a wise decision. In fact, I think it deserves a celebration. Let me take you somewhere fun tonight."

Fun. That was a foreign word to her until she arrived in Lavender Valley. She couldn't resist the invitation. "Yes, I'd love that."

"I'll pick you up around five if that works?"

"I'll be ready." She finished off her coffee and put her cup in the dishwasher. "I best get going. I promised Micki we'd work on labels for all the lavender treats I'm making for the festival and get that organized."

"That will be here before you know it." He carried her tote, while she took Vera and followed him to his truck.

The short trip took only minutes, and Heath left her with a long hug and the promise to see her soon. She put her things in the motorhome, and she and Vera came through the door to find Micki at the dining room table, already working on their project.

"Oh, I'm so glad you're home and all this nasty business is behind you." Micki rushed to greet her with a hug. "I'm having a cup of tea, if you'd like one."

Chief and Hope rushed to greet their tiniest friend, and she ran as fast as her legs would carry her to snuggle with them on the rug.

Micki put her pen down on a tablet. "I just spoke with the nicest lady, Kate, who lives in the San Juan Islands. She and three girlfriends want to come to the festival and wanted to book the paint and sip." Her smile widened. "All the slots are filled, so I couldn't resist inviting them to join us when Ashleigh comes on Thursday before the festival to do a dry-run for us. Kate was so appreciative, and now I can't wait to meet them. She even invited us to visit them, which sounds lovely."

"That will be fun, and those events are such a smart addition."

Micki pointed at the cardboard box on the table. "The packaging for our goodies arrived. I ordered a variety of the self-sealing cookie bags, craft bags, small boxes, and larger bags we can tie to close. We've got plenty of logo labels we can add to them. I just need your help to do the food labels correctly."

"We just have to list the ingredients, and note the normal allergens like milk, nuts, and so forth, plus have the name, address, and phone number of the farm. I'll start making a list for each product."

"That's great. I'll get started on some templates that will fit the bags and packaging, and we'll be in business. You've got your food handling class already and as long as we don't sell more than twenty thousand dollars each year, we don't need to have a license or inspection."

Lydia laughed. "I think we'll be safe this year. We're just restricted and can't sell anything that requires refrigeration, so if we want to expand, we'll have to go through the inspection process."

Micki nodded as she put stacks of bags and boxes on the table. "I think it makes sense to test it out this year. Get our feet wet, so to speak. Meg said she talked to Duke, and she's going to arrange her schedule at the clinic so she's off on Fridays and Saturdays to help during the festival."

"Oh, that's great news. I think we'll need all the help we can get." Lydia made a list of all the baked items she planned to make and the candies. "I think for the lemonades and iced teas, we can just put a sign up that says they're made in a kitchen with known allergens, including but not limited to eggs, dairy, nuts, wheat. Along with the disclaimer about being homemade and not in an inspected kitchen."

Micki shook her head. "I hope we can fit all that on our labels."

"I don't think there's a font size requirement." Lydia double checked her ingredient list for each item. "Oh, I decided not to go back to the Ranch House. I talked to Heath last night, and I think I need a break. Thinking about going back there and reliving the attack with Deidre was making me worry. So, that's good news in that I can focus on the festival, and we can get back to our Sunday family dinners."

"I can imagine going back would be stressful. Especially so soon. I know how much you love cooking, so I'm sure that wasn't easy for you, but I'm thrilled you'll be here more."

It took them the better part of the day to get the labels finalized. Olivia and Willow joined them after lunch and helped proofread.

As they wrapped up and neatly stacked the labels and packaging materials in a plastic bin, Lydia glanced at the time. "Heath's coming over around five. He said he's taking me somewhere fun to celebrate my new start at life without the fear of Marcus hanging over me."

Olivia grinned. "That sounds wonderful. Where are you going?"

"He wouldn't say. It's a surprise."

Micki slid Lydia's list of products into the bin and snapped the lid shut. "Oh, that's even more fun. He's a great guy. It's my turn to cook tonight, and I was going to ask you to invite Heath. Buck, Duke, and Clay are joining us. But, it sounds like you have a much better offer of a night out."

Lydia blushed. "I'm sort of excited. I've never felt this way before. Maybe in high school. There was this guy I thought was so cute, Charlie. I can't even remember his last name now, but sometimes, I'd lose track of what the teacher was saying because I was staring at him. I thought he was gorgeous and all that, you know?"

Micki chuckled. "We've all been there. That weak-in-the-knees feeling. Steve had that effect on me until the day I lost him."

"At my age, I thought that part of my life was over, but Duke brought that spark back." Olivia glanced over at Lydia.

"I can tell by the way Heath looks at you that he truly cares about you. If I didn't know better, I'd say he's smitten."

Smitten might be an old-fashioned word, but it was the perfect one to describe Lydia's feelings for Heath. Her heart beat quicker. "Well, I better get ready. I have no idea what to wear."

Micki pointed up the stairs. "You're welcome to go through my closet and take whatever works."

"Oh, how fun," said Olivia. "Yes, go through anything I have, too. We need a fashion show."

Lydia hurried upstairs and started in Micki's room. A flutter sleeve shirt in a gorgeous blue-green color that made her think of the ocean caught her eye. She also took a black blouse that looked dressier, and Micki insisted she try a pair of lightweight white pants.

In Olivia's room, she found a cute white denim jacket and a pretty open-weave sweater with subtle glitter woven into the yarn that matched the flutter sleeve shirt. The two of them waited in the hallway, while Lydia tried things on.

She emerged wearing the white pants with the black blouse first. Lydia twirled around and laughed. Both of them liked the outfit, and Lydia liked the crisscross style straps at the neckline.

Next, she tried the blue shirt and popped the lightweight short cardigan over it. She came out of the bedroom and modeled it, pretending she was on a runway and turning for her two judges. Then she hurried back and replaced the sweater with the white denim jacket.

Olivia and Micki clapped and laughed. Lydia's heart overflowed with joy. All these years of longing for a family, for sisters, this was what she dreamed. Micki hurried to her room and returned with two pairs of sandals. She held them up for Lydia. "Olivia and Harry both have giant feet, so there's no chance anything they have will fit you, but these might work."

She slipped on the tan pair with the slight wedge. They looked great with her jeans and were super comfy. She took another look in the full-length mirror on the bathroom door. "I think I like this with the sweater best. I love that black blouse, but it feels sort of too fancy. Like I'm trying too hard."

Micki and Olivia bobbed their heads. "You look great in that," said Micki.

"Either works, but this look is definitely more casual, and I think you're right; the sweater is a great match."

Lydia gazed at her reflection once more. "Are you sure you're okay with me borrowing this stuff?"

Micki rolled her eyes. "Of course we are."

Olivia nodded. "I think you should get rid of the ponytail and wear your hair down. It's gorgeous."

She couldn't resist hugging both of them before she hurried out to the motorhome to finish getting ready.

After fiddling with her hair for longer than she expected, she put on some blush and mascara, gave her lips a swish of gloss, and slipped into Micki's sandals. As she came through the mudroom door, Heath's truck pulled into the driveway.

Lydia hurried to give Olivia and Micki a quick twirl of the finished look. They both grinned and clapped their hands together. "You look gorgeous," said Micki, as she worked on placing tortillas in a baking dish.

"Perfection," said Olivia.

Heath knocked on the door, and Lydia opened it, taking in his tall frame dressed in a light-blue button down and jeans. She was glad she picked the casual shirt and sweater. His blue eyes flickered. "You look beautiful, Lydia."

She blushed and reached for her purse, giving Vera a pet

on the head. He ducked around the dining room table and said, "Hello, ladies."

Olivia looked up from the sink. "Looking sharp, Heath."

He chuckled. "Thank you. We probably won't be back until after ten."

Micki wiped her hands on a towel. "You guys have fun."

He raised his brows at Lydia. "Ready?"

She nodded and went through the door and down the porch steps. He held the passenger door for her and then got behind the wheel. As he started the truck, he said, "So, it's down the road about twelve miles, so it won't take long."

"Hmm, still not telling me where we're going."

"Nah, I like surprises." He laughed and accelerated down the highway.

She soaked in the beauty of the green fields and wildflowers that lined the highway as they drove by farms and acreage. Within a few minutes, Heath turned off the highway, and they crossed the Applegate River. He steered the truck along a tree-lined driveway, and she saw the sign for Red River Vineyards.

She'd never heard of it, but as the property came into view, her mouth hung open. Nestled in the valley, the beautiful vineyard framed wooden buildings with shiny red metal roofs. Tall trees and lush green lawns framed the buildings, and cheerful red umbrellas dotted the large patios surrounding the buildings while music filled the air.

He parked the truck and turned to her. "Surprise," he said, with that slow grin.

"This looks fabulous. What a gorgeous setting."

He hopped out of the truck and went around to her side, taking her hand and holding it while they made their way to the entrance. He gave his name to the young woman at the welcome table, and she handed them two wristbands. "Enjoy your evening."

After they slipped their wristbands on, Heath looped his arm in Lydia's and led her past the retail area and indoor tables to the French doors on the side of the stone fireplace that dominated the back wall. Once outside, she noticed the fireplace was two sided and usable from the patio as well.

Tables were scattered on the large patio, with more positioned in the grass that led down to the river. Next door was a pole barn, done in the same gorgeous wood and red metal roof. Large wooden tables and benches were positioned along the wide concrete that surrounded the unique building. Heath pointed at the barn. "They restored an old pole barn from the 1920s and made it into a tasting room."

He led her over to it, where festive lights were strung along the thick beams. She glanced up at the tall, open ceiling, laced with wooden trusses where more lights glowed. Wine barrels were stacked in wooden shelves along the exterior walls, and more wooden tables and benches filled the interior space.

She loved the rustic vibe and warmth the wood provided. Heath pointed outside. "They've got a small stage set up by the river and more tables. They have live music events most weekends all summer." He pointed at his wristbands. "These entitle us to free food and drinks, plus the music. They've got appetizers and snacks, wood-fire pizzas, and a couple of sandwiches. It's pretty simple, but good."

He led them out of the barn. "I'll give you the lay of the land, and then we can pick a place to sit."

As they walked to the edge of the largest patio, she pointed at the table with built-in narrow glass fire pits. They were positioned with a perfect view of the river that would allow them to see the stage. "Oh, can we sit at one of those?"

"Excellent choice. We can still hear the music, but it won't be so loud up here."

He chose a table with only two chairs and held hers out for her. As soon as he sat, a server wearing a red apron came to the table. "Welcome to Red River," she said, setting glasses of iced water in front of them.

She handed them a small menu attached to a red leather holder. "I can give you a few minutes and bring you a tasting flight if you'd like to try our wines before making your selection."

"Sounds great, thanks," said Heath, letting Lydia read the offerings. As the server left, he pointed at the selection of wines. "They're a small winery and concentrate on Spanish varieties. Most all are reds, with the exception of this Verdejo."

Lydia smiled. "I'm not familiar with many Spanish wines, so I think I'll have to taste them to make my choice." She glanced at the food selections. "I think the tapas platter and a pizza sound good to me."

"I'll get a panini, and we can split it and the pizza," said Heath.

The server returned with a flight of wines for each of them. While Lydia delighted in the presentation of the wine in test tubes in wooden racks, Heath placed their food order and asked for iced tea.

Lydia took her first taste of their bestselling red and smiled. "That's good." She kept at it and after trying them all, decided on deep garnet red. "I love the hint of plum and boysenberry in this."

He smiled at her, and she raised her brows. "What?"

"Lydia," he said, his voice soft.

The way he said her name, and the look in his blue eyes, left her breathless.

"You're even more beautiful when you smile." He leaned closer and held her chin with his thumb, while he skimmed his lips over hers.

Her head swam, and her legs tingled. She hadn't drunk enough wine to have that effect. It was all Heath.

Tonight was shaping up to be the best one she'd had in a very long time.

CHAPTER TWENTY-THREE

As the flames danced before them, Heath slipped his arm around Lydia's shoulders. She gazed at the slow river winding through the property and the low hills beyond it. The stress of the last week melted away as she sipped her wine.

The server returned with their food and another glass of wine for Lydia. After a few sips from his tasting flight, Heath stuck with iced tea since he was driving. As they snacked on grapes, cheese, pieces of fresh baguette, and flavorful salami and prosciutto, the performers took to the stage.

They were a regional band, with the main vocalist playing an acoustic guitar. They played old rock and country hits that had the crowd tapping their toes, with many couples dancing in the grass along the river.

As the sun disappeared and the sky darkened, they held hands and swayed to the music. Lydia rested her head on Heath's shoulder and let the tranquility of the scenery wash over her. Soon, the band announced their last song for the evening.

Heath bumped his shoulder against hers. "Dance with me?"

She couldn't refuse and took his hand. He led her down to the flat area of the grass along the river, and the band began to play "We Danced," as several couples moved to the easy rhythm.

Lydia leaned against Heath and breathed in the scent of citrus and fresh-cut grass along his neck. In the arms of the man she was falling deeper in love with, she was lost in the lyrics. Lost in the moment. She didn't want the evening to end.

As the last notes of the song drifted away with the breeze, she kept her arms around Heath. As couples around them left, and the band packed up their instruments, Heath released his arms and reached for her hand.

"Come with me." He tilted his head towards the pathway along the river. They followed the glow from the lights along the edges of the path, and he led her around the bend. He led them off the main path, where paper luminaries glowed and flickered, lighting their way to a bench nestled beneath the trees.

Twinkle lights crisscrossed above and were strung around the edges of the bench. He held her hand as she took a seat, and then he sat next to her. Steps away, the river swirled and splashed over rocks, and the velvet sky above them twinkled with stars.

Lydia leaned her head back and against Heath's arm, and she gazed at the heavens. "It's breathtaking out here," she whispered.

"I'm glad you like it. I brought you here, well, because I have something special to ask you. He reached in his pocket and across the pathway, next to the water, more lights came to life, and Lydia gulped as she realized they spelled out MARRY ME?

Heath fumbled with his other pocket and extracted a small velvet box. He kneeled in front of her, his eyes sparkling in the warm lights above them. "Lydia, I realized today when you were leaving that I didn't want you to go. I know we've only known each other a short time, but you're what's been missing from my life. I don't want to add more stress to your life right now, but I would love for you to be my wife and spend the rest of our lives together. We don't need to set a date or even think about a wedding right away, but I couldn't wait another minute to ask you and tell you just how very much I love you."

His words sucked all the breath from her lungs. Her heart was pounding, and her palms were slick with sweat. "I never dreamed this was what you had planned." She smiled at him and placed her hands along the sides of his face. "I love you, too. Yes, I'll marry you, Heath Nolan. How could I refuse all this?"

He chuckled. "Now, there is one condition. We have to stay here in Lavender Valley."

"I can't imagine ever leaving."

He leaned forward and brought his lips to hers. After a long, deep kiss, he broke away and slipped the ring on her finger. Lydia gasped as the diamond flickered in the light. "So, this diamond was one of my mother's. The day I met you, I think I knew you were the one. I took it to a jeweler we've known for years and had him make an engagement and wedding band out of mom's necklace. He said to come to see him if you need it sized. We just guessed."

She ran her hand over it. it was smooth all the way around. "I think it's okay, but we can take a closer look in the daylight."

He hugged her closely. "I'm just so glad you said yes, and I didn't scare you away." He slid back on the bench next to her and put his arm around her. "I asked Clay what he thought, and he convinced me not to let a chance at happiness slip through my fingers. I know I don't want to have a life without you in it, and I want to spend the rest of my days here, with you."

She leaned her head on his shoulder. "I never imagined I'd meet the man of my dreams next door to Jewel's farm. She's still working her magic."

He kissed the top of her head. "I only wish we could share it with her."

She glanced up at the sky. "Somehow, I think she knows."

When Heath walked her to the door, all the dogs stared at them through the glass, tails wagging in welcome. He left her with a long embrace, and she came through the door to find Olivia, Harry, and Micki, all still awake, sitting on the couch and watching television.

She picked up Vera and joined her sisters, squeezing between Olivia and Micki. She made a production of using her left hand and flashing the ring at them. Harry hit the pause button on the remote. "Is that what I think it is?" She grabbed Lydia's hand.

Lydia grinned and laughed. "Heath proposed to me tonight."

Micki and Olivia squealed with delight, each of them vying for a look at the ring. "That's gorgeous," said Olivia, holding her hand and then passing it over to Micki.

"Oh, beautiful. I like that modern look and the square cut of the diamond."

Lydia stared at it. "I normally don't wear any jewelry in the kitchen, but this one may work. The main stone and the accents are all bezel set, so it's totally smooth with nothing to catch on anything. I just don't want to lose it."

They all hugged her and congratulated her. "Do you have a date yet?" asked Micki.

Lydia shook her head. "No, we're not in a rush. Heath said he just couldn't wait and didn't want to take the chance I'd decide to jump in Gypsy and hit the road one day. He wanted me to know this was my home forever."

"Aww," said Olivia, bringing her hand on her chest. "He's a sweetheart."

"You two are a great match. Imagine the kitchen competitions you'll have." Harry laughed and reached down to pet Hope and Chief, who were leaning against her legs.

Olivia grinned. "This calls for a proper celebration. I'm going to call May in the morning and see what we can put together. I'm so happy for you, Lydia. I can't think of anyone who deserves such happiness more than you."

CHAPTER TWENTY-FOUR

After Lydia got home from the market on Monday, she put away the groceries, and her mind wandered to thoughts of being married to Heath.

Sunday morning, he and Clay invited all of them over to the ranch, along with Duke's family, for an impromptu brunch to celebrate their engagement. He insisted Lydia do nothing but sit on the patio, drink mimosas, and let her new ring glitter in the sunshine.

She smiled just thinking about him. He made her laugh and made her feel safe and loved. Those three things had been missing from her life for several years. It took being here, surrounded by her supportive sisters and a loving community, to see what was right in front of her. Like Heath said, she'd been existing, but she hadn't been living.

Heath couldn't stop grinning at her or at the mention of her name. When Clay looked at her ring and hugged her, he thanked her for making his brother happy and told her how excited he was to have her as part of their family.

Along with all the smiles, Lydia shed a few tears, listening to the kind words of her family and friends. Several times, she thought it was all just a dream. A lovely dream, but she'd wake up in Gypsy and not have a ring on her finger, having hallucinated the whole thing.

Heath captured several photos of the lights the winery rigged up for him at the proposal site and passed his phone around the table so everyone could check it out. May wrapped her good arm around Heath's neck while he was cooking and told him what a good job he'd done setting up the perfect spot for his proposal. He even blushed a bit when she kissed his cheek and congratulated him.

He and Clay both said how much their parents would have loved to meet Lydia and be part of the celebration and how happy they would be that Heath found the love of his life.

Lydia had been so caught up in the moment and the romantic proposal, floating on a cloud, she hadn't considered any of the practicalities, but alone now with her thoughts, they were front and center in her mind.

Heath would never leave the ranch, so she assumed they'd live there after they were married. She wondered how Clay would feel about that. Although, with the size of that place, you could have eight people living in the house and never see each other. She hated the idea of disrupting their home or their relationship.

The idea of never having to run again and spending her days with a man like Heath made her toes tingle. Not to mention, cooking in that kitchen of theirs. When she'd arrived last month, broke and running low on hope and energy, she never expected to stay long. She never imagined she'd find all she'd been missing.

Her sisters of the heart and Jewel's farm were her chance to rest while she figured out where she'd go next. As she gazed upon Jewel's kitchen and remembered all the happy times with her, a tear slid down her cheek. She hated the idea of leaving Lavender Valley, and Heath hadn't only declared his love and promised a life together, but he'd also given the best gift of all. A real home surrounded by all she held dear and the chance to put down roots. Real roots.

As she pictured what it would be like living at the ranch and what would happen to Jewel's farm after this year, anxiety invaded her thoughts. She took a deep breath. She was getting way ahead of herself. Like Heath said, they didn't need to be in a hurry and with the festival coming, she had more than enough to keep her busy.

She went about dicing the tomatoes and red onions, adding in chopped, fresh basil, minced garlic, oregano, salt and pepper, and a healthy splash of olive oil. She mixed it all together to let the flavors blend. She took a whiff from the bowl. It smelled divine.

The chicken breasts were seasoned and wouldn't take long to grill. All that was left was to boil the pasta for the bruschetta salad she planned for their dinner.

Last night, May and Janet invited all the ladies to Cranberry Cottage for a small private party to wrap their special lavender soaps for the festival and celebrate Lydia's engagement with some snacks and drinks. While they were there, they put in a video call to Georgia to share the good news. Harry already booked a reservation at Wine and Words, the new wine bar and bookstore downtown, so the five sisters could celebrate Georgia's homecoming and Lydia's engagement together when Georgia got to town.

Georgia's doctor wanted to see her for one more checkup, but she was tentatively planning to arrive the last week of June. She assured them her shoulder was feeling better, and she would be on hand to help with the festival.

When Georgia mentioned her late husband, grief clouded her eyes. She brightened when they discussed the festival and the farm. Returning to Lavender Valley and meeting her sisters of the heart gave Georgia something to look forward to and made her smile.

Lydia already loved her, just from their video calls. She reminded Lydia of Jewel. She had a softness about her and those same maternal instincts as Jewel. She always wanted to hear about all of them and what they were doing. She laughed at Olivia's stories about the dogs and the goats and couldn't wait to meet all the animals.

When Lydia shared her news about Heath's proposal, Georgia beamed with excitement. She longed to be part of the fun and couldn't wait to set eyes on her new fiancé.

Last night, she told them she had more goat pajamas to bring with her and made a few more aprons and table runners. She'd left the ladies with air kisses and best wishes for Lydia and Heath, counting the days until she'd see them all in person.

Lydia had the house to herself and with her prep work for dinner done, she tried to keep from watching the clock. Harry told her Marcus was due in court at three o'clock and promised to call the moment she knew anything.

Micki and Meg were in Medford to visit Jade, and Olivia was delivering Thelma and Milton to their new forever home. An older couple who lived in Applegate, just down the road from the winery she and Heath visited, fell in love with them from their online photos and came to meet them over the past weekend. After checking their references, Olivia approved the adoption, and she and the other dogs, including Vera, were taking a road trip to deliver them.

As Lydia thought of Vera and how happy she was being part of a pack and how she loved romping around with her big cousin dogs, her heart swelled. Like Lydia, she wouldn't have to leave ever again. She could live out her life surrounded by her family and friends, running through the lavender fields.

A few minutes before four o'clock, Harry's SUV pulled in front of the house. She came up the steps and tossed her bag on the bench by the door. "Hey," she said, striding into the kitchen. "The court was running behind. Just got word from Salem; the judge denied bail, so Marcus is staying put behind bars for the time being."

Lydia let out a long breath and rushed to Harry to hug her. "Thank you. I'm so relieved." She turned toward the fridge. "I was just going to pour myself some iced tea. Want one?"

"Sounds perfect. It's been a long day."

Lydia joined Harry in the living room, where she was stretched out on the sofa. "As much as I was telling myself it didn't matter, waiting for the ruling on the bail was eating at me."

Harry took a long swallow. "They've been working all weekend and think Marcus is tied to another murder. This one is in Portland from fifteen years ago. His DNA is a preliminary match to that from a case where a woman was found raped and strangled in the same park where they found Claudia. They've got to rerun the old evidence, since our technology has improved so much."

Lydia covered her mouth as she gasped. "Oh, my gosh. He is worse than I ever imagined."

Harry nodded. "They're still working on the case but presented the preliminary results in court and let the judge know more charges will be forthcoming. The guys watching in court said Marcus looked defeated. A couple nights in jail has worn the shine off him."

"I'm sure he figured he could buy his way out of this." Lydia shook her head. "When I think about Claudia and now this other woman, I realize how lucky I was to get away from him. I was so dumb to ever trust him."

"He's a predator. They're skilled at hunting and manipulation. Like you said, the minute he's denied what he wants, or his charm and manipulation fails, things escalate, and he becomes violent. He needs to be locked up for life."

"As much as I'm not a fan of Deidre and worried she would kill me, I think in a way, she was his prisoner. I hope he pays for his crimes."

"The detectives are beating the bushes at the legislature and turning up some women who have some stories about Marcus. I'm not sure they'll amount to much in the criminal case, but his list of friends and protectors is shrinking by the minute. Those in political circles are scurrying to distance themselves and insulate their reputations. Soon, he'll be on an island."

"He's going to have a hard time not being in control."

"Criminals like him, the ones who are the biggest bullies and tormentors, are the ones who are the weakest once they're confronted and challenged with facts and evidence and facing real consequences. They usually end up crying in the interview room, begging for mercy. His fake and pretentious world he lived in is crumbling around him, and the realization will be sinking in soon."

Lydia couldn't wait to sit in a courtroom and watch him squirm.

CHAPTER TWENTY-FIVE

Tuesday morning, Lydia and Vera descended the steps of the motorhome and wandered along the lavender fields before heading to the house. Bees buzzed among the vivid purple buds and blooms. While Vera explored, Lydia admired the sight of the purple fields stretching across the land. She inhaled the lovely scent and wished Jewel were here.

She would be overjoyed to see the girls she loved forming a family. Her beloved dog rescue program was thriving under Olivia's competent hands, and Micki had once again proven to be magnificent in her ability to expand the lavender business while tending to the plants and garden, all while working remotely.

Harry being elected as mayor of Jewel's beloved valley would delight her to no end and with Harry's profound ability to solve problems and take charge of any situation, it probably wouldn't even surprise her. Seeing the men Jewel admired and loved to become a huge and important part of their lives, would fill her heart with such happiness. Jewel adored Duke, trusted Buck, and thought of Clay and Heath as her own sons.

Lydia longed to sit with her and sip tea in the kitchen and tell her all about Heath's proposal and how she finally felt whole with him. A part of her had been damaged and empty for so long and like any frailty, she'd learned to live with it. The wound deep inside that had been there since she was a child had grown when her mother went to prison.

The years Lydia spent at the farm with Jewel and Chuck had healed that lesion and by nurturing her love of cooking and creating, Jewel restored Lydia's confidence and gave her a purpose. Marcus had effectively worked to destroy it and reopened the old wound, while inflicting a few new ones.

Now, Jewel had orchestrated another chance for Lydia. She brought her home, to her sisters of the heart, who through their love and support, convinced her she was worthy of more. She'd never had a circle of friends like those who gathered on Sunday morning to shower her and Heath with their love and best wishes.

Since her time at Jewel's, Lydia had been on her own, with Jewel's support through calls and letters, but nobody she could turn to on a daily basis. For a few years, she thought if she found the right guy, she could make her own family. They could have children, and she could be a mom, maybe work part time. As the years ticked by, that dream vanished. The few men she chose to let into her life, to trust, had proven to be horrible. Marcus was the last in a string of bad choices, and he was by far the worst.

After her decision to flee Portland and keep moving for fear of being found, thinking too far ahead was impossible. It was too hard. Too distressing and depressing. She had no future. No hope. If she gave it too much thought, it would incapacitate her. Instead, she used mental gymnastics and made it seem like a fun game. Where would she go next? She tried to embrace the adventure.

She couldn't let herself get too attached to people, because she would be moving on in a few months. She kept herself at a distance, never divulging much, always leery of anyone who paid her too much attention.

As she stared at the hills in the distance and the perfect summer sky above, she took a deep breath. Here, she could relax. Here, she could build the life she only dreamed about so long ago. It was too late for children, but she had a family of her own and a man who loved her and wanted to build a life together.

She hadn't given much thought to their wedding. She only knew it would be the happiest day of her life, but also bittersweet without Jewel there to share it. The idea of being the center of attention made her stomach churn. She hoped Heath would be open to a small ceremony. Maybe they could do it at the ranch.

Vera brushing against her legs jarred her from her daydreams. She bent and picked her up. "Shall we get you some breakfast?"

Surprised at how far she'd wandered, Lydia turned and headed back to the house, her hungry dog anxious for the meal she promised.

They wandered to the mudroom, where she found Vera's little bowl already waiting for her. Courtesy of Olivia, no doubt. The kindness of her sisters tugged at her heart. Lydia placed it on the floor and left Vera to enjoy it.

Drawn by the aroma of freshly brewed coffee, Lydia wandered into the kitchen. She poured a cup and turned to find all of her sisters sitting at the dining room table.

"Morning," she said, carrying her cup to join them. She noticed their somber faces. "What's going on?"

Harry set her cup on the table. "I got a call this morning from my old boss in Salem. When they did their morning checks, they found Marcus in his cell dead. He hanged himself."

Lydia gasped and, with a trembling hand, set her cup on a napkin. "Wow, I would never guess he'd do that." She shook her head. "It almost seems too easy. I mean that sounds bad, he's dead after all. I guess I wanted to see him face his crimes in court."

Harry arched her brows. "For someone with as big an ego as his, I'm not sure he could do it. When we talked about his world crumbling around him, I think it really was. All the politicians he knew and worked for over his career abandoned him. He was suddenly persona non grata."

Olivia refilled her cup of tea. "I'm sure he realized he didn't have a chance of beating the charges, especially with more cases coming to light. From what you've said about him, Lydia, he thrived on power and control. He most likely saw his ability to dominate slipping away, and suicide was his last way to control things."

Harry nodded. "I think so too, Olivia. I'm sure he couldn't face spending the rest of his life in prison."

Micki put her hand on Lydia's arm. "Are you okay?"

"Yeah." She nodded. "It's surreal in a way. The person I feared more than anything is gone. I'm relieved for sure, but it's disappointing he won't have to answer for his crimes."

She took a sip from her cup. "I've also been thinking about Deidre. I have mixed feelings about her. I've been considering writing a statement, so the judge knows I don't hold her totally responsible for the attack."

Harry tilted her head. "Her psych evaluation will take weeks, and I'm convinced she'll never stand trial for anything. I don't think she's fit, and I'm sure she's not faking it. She's mentally ill and will probably spend her life in an institution."

"Medication and therapy might help her," said Olivia. "It's hard to know, and it sounds like she's been untreated for decades, which makes the outlook grim."

Micki's shoulder slumped. "It breaks my heart that she was in the foster system. She obviously didn't have a great life and then gets placed with a family like Marcus'. They and the system failed Deidre in a catastrophic way."

Lydia bit her bottom lip. "It makes you realize how lucky we all were. Jewel was a rare treasure in the foster system. If not for her, any one of us could have ended up in a place like Deidre. It makes me sick when I think about her life with them and knowing what Marcus was capable of. We know some of what he did to her, but I can imagine it's worse than we think."

Harry leaned back in her chair. "In so many cases, there are no happy endings. I'm afraid this is one of them."

Micki glanced over at Lydia. "As hard as it is, I hope you can put this behind you and embrace the future with Heath. In a way, it might be good to have this chapter closed, even though it means not having all the answers. You won't have the trial hanging over you or have to worry about reporters seeking information. The news cycle will forget Marcus and your attack and move on to the next shiny object."

Lydia smiled at her. "You're right. The idea of reliving my time with him or being associated with him at all is repulsive. I was focused on seeing him face his crimes and his victims but hadn't considered the press coverage."

Harry rose and took her empty cup to the kitchen. "I don't think you would have gotten the answers you were looking for in court. His lawyer would have never put him on the stand. He would have been working for a plea deal to avoid court."

Lydia traced the rim of her cup with her finger. "Like Micki said, I need to close this chapter and be glad it's over."

The dogs running to the front door announced Heath before his boots clomped across the porch. He knocked on the door, and Harry opened it with a wave toward the dining room. "Come on in, we're all in here."

He strode to the table and smiled. "Morning, ladies." He walked behind Lydia's chair and put his hands on her shoulders. "I came to whisk my bride-to-be away."

Lydia tilted her head back and looked up at him. "Where are we going?"

"It's a surprise." He winked at her, and her heart melted.

Olivia picked up Vera and put her on her lap. "I'll watch over Vera. You go and enjoy yourself."

Heath took her by the hand and led her to the porch. He pointed at the two horses tied to the railing. "Your chariot awaits." He held up a pair of cowboy boots. "You'll need to wear these."

A twinge of fear rose in her throat as she pulled on the boots. He tugged on her hand. "Come on, I won't let anything happen to you. You won't find a gentler horse than Merlot." He grinned and kissed her cheek. "It's a new adventure, and it'll be fun, I promise."

With more reassurance, he brought her around the left side of the horse and got her up and in the saddle, made sure she balanced herself, and that the balls of her feet were in the stirrups. She looked at the ground and winced. It was a long way down.

Heath took her hand and encouraged her to lean forward and pet Merlot. "Just talk nice to her. She knows you're scared."

He explained the reins were for steering the horse and that she probably wouldn't even need to use them much; Merlot needed very little direction. He demonstrated the tension needed, which wasn't much, to tell the horse to stop. He showed her where to squeeze with her legs to get Merlot to move forward, stressing again a gentle pressure.

He reached over to his horse and retrieved a buckskin-colored hat and motioned Lydia to bend down. He placed it on her head and tightened the chin strap. He stood back and gazed at her. "That was one of my mom's favorite hats, and you are gorgeous in it."

Lydia's heart fluttered, with both nerves and affection. With an effortless movement, Heath mounted his horse, Crown Royal, and reached his hand out to Lydia. "We'll go slow, don't worry."

He set off at a slow pace and as he promised, Merlot didn't need any direction from her. She simply walked alongside Crown Royal. The motion reminded her of a gentle sway. Heath encouraged her to relax and move with Merlot, as if they were one.

After they went past the lavender fields, Heath picked up the pace, and Merlot did the same. It was a slow trot instead of a slow walk. Heath pointed at the saddle horn. "Hold onto that if you feel you need it, but don't pull on the reins to steady yourself."

Trotting was odd at first, but as they continued, Lydia relaxed, mindful to keep her legs from squeezing Merlot and let them hang, with her weight on her heels. Heath encouraged her to relax as she bounced along the pathway.

"We'll work on posting, which is when you rise slightly out of the saddle to keep from bouncing with the horse's movements. It takes some practice."

He reminded her to sit up tall and straight and look

through Merlot's ears. By the time they reached the creek, Lydia's unease was gone.

Heath pointed at the creek. "We're going to cross it at a narrow and shallow spot. Merlot is used to it, so don't be afraid. I'll be right next to you, and we'll just go slowly through the water."

Every muscle in her body tightened. "Just relax," Heath reminded her. "Merlot has done this thousands of times and knows what to do. Hold the saddle horn to steady yourself."

The creek was only a few feet across and as Heath promised, it was an easy crossing, and the horses took them out of the water to the grove of trees not far from the edge.

Heath dismounted and tied Crown Royal to a hitching post, then turned his attention to Lydia. He guided her in kicking her feet loose from the stirrups and keeping hold of the reins. Since Merlot was experienced and wouldn't wander off, he had Lydia hold the saddle horn while she leaned forward, swung her right leg toward the back of the horse, and slid down the side.

Heath held her by the waist. "Good job. Now, your legs might feel a bit weak since you're not used to riding. That will go away."

They stood for a few minutes, and he took her hand. She moved the brim of her hat up so she could see his eyes. "Now that we're going to be married, I don't think we should have any secrets." Her face was serious as she met his eyes.

He nodded. "Okay, but now you're scaring me."

"It is serious." She nodded. "I need you to know..." She stopped and shook her head. "This is really hard for me."

"Whatever it is, it doesn't matter."

She took a deep breath. "I need you to know, I never turned in my chili in the cookoff." She couldn't keep up the pretense and burst out laughing.

He grinned and tilted her hat all the way back against her neck and kissed her. "You got me. So, you let me win? That hurts." He feigned grasping at his heart.

"You were having a bad day, and I thought you needed a boost."

He reached for her hand, still chuckling as he led her to the bench under the trees. "This was my mom and dad's favorite place." He touched the engraving on the back of the bench. "Clay and I made this for their twenty-fifth wedding anniversary."

He squeezed her hand and gestured for her to sit with him.

She sighed as she leaned against the back of it. "Did you hear the news about Marcus?"

He nodded. "Harry called and told me about it this morning. I thought you could use a distraction."

She chuckled. "I have to admit, sitting up there on Merlot, I didn't think about him or the whole ordeal once. I was too focused on not falling off or messing up."

He grinned. "My plan worked." He pointed at the area behind the grove of trees. "Actually, I brought you here because this is where my mom and dad are interred. This was their place, and they wanted to spend eternity here."

She gazed at the green hills. "I can see why. It's a stunning spot."

"It sounds weird, but I come here sometimes when I need to talk to them. I rode out here that day I decided to propose. I wanted them to know first."

She saw the glint of tears in his eyes. "While I wish they were still here to meet you and get to know you, I wanted to share this place with you." His voice cracked. "Share them with you."

She lifted his hand with hers and placed it against her

chest. "That means the world to me, Heath. I was thinking this morning how much I wish Jewel was here to see us together. To be at our wedding. I know you feel that same way about your parents."

"So much. I'm looking at the bright side that I'll be able to include Cassidy. She's a welcome surprise in my life, and I was hoping you could come over tonight, and we could video chat with her and share the big news. We should have done that Sunday, but in all the excitement, I forgot. I'm still not used to having a daughter, I guess."

"I'd love to call her with you, and we'll have to plan the wedding when it works for her to visit."

He slipped his hand from hers and put his arm around her shoulder. "I was thinking a small wedding, maybe at the ranch. Just family and a few friends."

She leaned her head on his shoulder and sighed, content to let him ramble on about wedding plans and horses.

Along with the comfort and safety she sought, she'd found so much more in Lavender Valley.

Life.

Love.

Family.

EPILOGUE

Georgia turned off the highway for Lavender Valley. Her eight-hour drive from Boise had turned into almost ten hours, and she was beyond tired. After begging her doctor to release her to make the drive, he finally caved but made her promise to stop every two hours to walk and give her shoulder some rest.

He didn't want her stuck in the driving position for hours on end. She promised to follow his advice, and Georgia was always true to her word. She was so excited to get to the farm and meet all of her new sisters. The video calls were wonderful, but there was nothing like a real hug.

Lydia was making dinner, and the idea of a good meal, and a hot shower sounded heavenly. Georgia drove along the road she remembered from so long ago. The last time she'd been to Lavender Valley had been with Lee, more than twenty years ago. Tears clouded her eyes.

Her thoughts drifted to Jewel. Before her death, she knew of Lee's passing, but she had no idea of the state he left things and Georgia's predicament. Georgia was still coming to grips with it, and the last thing she wanted to do was worry Jewel, who was struggling with her health.

Had Harry's letter not arrived, Georgia wasn't sure what she would have done or where she would be. Lavender Valley Farm had saved her once, and now it would save her again. Thankful for a place to stay while she healed and figured out what she was going to do, Georgia was looking forward to sharing her days with her newfound sisters of the heart. She only wished Jewel would be there to greet her.

Tears blurred her vision, and she willed her mind to focus on the positive. While her shoulder injury was a huge setback, connecting with her sisters of the heart helped her find a purpose. She made good use of her downtime and after video chatting with her sisters, poured her energy into creating items for the Lavender Festival. Her car was loaded down with table runners, placemats, wall hangings, and more. Her trusty sewing machine was carefully wrapped and boxed, resting in the backseat.

As she made the final turn into Lavender Valley, her heart filled with both joy and regret. The quaint feel of Main Street, which hadn't changed much since her first visit almost fifty years ago, welcomed her. She only wished she had found time to visit Jewel more often. Now, it was too late.

At the sight of the Sugar Shack, she could almost taste the warm cinnamon rolls she loved, and the windows of Cranberry Cottage, filled with gorgeous offerings nestled among flowers and vintage furniture, made her want to stop. Her smile widened when she spotted the fabric and yarn store. She longed to spend time looking through the bolts and skeins. There was no point though. Her funds were low, and she didn't have the freedom to buy anything but the necessities.

The cost of the movers had been a stretch, but it was behind her and like Lee always used to say, everything would be okay. No matter what, the stars would shine tonight, and the sun would rise tomorrow. He also always said they'd have each other. His words had always comforted her in times of doubt, but now he was gone and so was his promise.

He'd been a kind and good man. A wonderful husband and partner. He cherished Georgia, and she missed him terribly. He'd always handled everything, and Georgia was content to let him take care of her. He had given her everything she craved. Love, a home, a purpose. The almost forty years they shared had been wonderful. The only real sadness she'd endured was their inability to have children.

That hole in her life led Georgia to admire Jewel and her selfless mothering of foster children even more. Georgia had longed for her own family for years. At one time, she considered becoming a foster parent, but with Lee's job as a teacher, he'd seen too much failure and heartbreak in the broken system and wanted nothing to do with it.

Over time, they'd learned to accept their fate and poured their parental instincts into guiding the students who crossed their paths each day at school. When they retired only a few years ago, they had big plans to travel more and enjoy their golden years.

Everything changed with Lee's illness. He failed so quickly, and the hope they held faded in a matter of weeks. Looking back, she now realized he'd been trying to tell her. He looked at her with such pleading in his eyes, and he was too weak to get the words out. She'd assumed he was worried about leaving her and reassured him she would be okay.

She didn't know what she would learn after his death. Over the last few months, she'd relied on Jewel's words, reminding Georgia she was strong and capable. Georgia's early life had taught her there was no point in crying or shriveling into despair. Life wasn't fair or easy. Sixty years later, the same was true.

After assessing the facts and reality, Georgia was left with little choice and a very uncertain future. Until Harry's letter arrived. The chance she'd been searching for had arrived in the kind words of that short invitation. Now, she had hope again and at least the rest of the year to figure out a new path forward.

Without the promise of connecting with her new sisters and the possibilities that came with a new adventure in Lavender Valley, Georgia couldn't have gotten through the last hard months.

Saying goodbye to the home she loved broke her heart. It was like tossing all her memories and life with Lee out the window. Prior to Harry's letter, Georgia was lost and looking for solutions. Now, she was driving down the street where she walked countless times, seeing the same buildings and reminders from her youth.

There was such comfort in the familiar surroundings. The planters overflowing with colorful blooms and the slow pace of the cars making their way down the street, stopping for pedestrians and waiting for cars to back out of parking spots, warmed her heart.

She caught a glimpse of a woman with a young girl walking a dog past City Hall. It was like stepping back into a kinder and gentler time. Georgia needed that right now. She longed for a soft place to heal and not only did Lavender Valley offer that, but it held the promise of the family she'd always wanted.

The sisters she never knew were waiting for her just down the road. She pressed the accelerator when she reached the highway. She couldn't wait to meet them and get settled before the Lavender Festival kicked off in a couple of weeks.

———

Continue Georgia's story in REUNION IN LAVENDER VALLEY, the next book in the series.

Don't miss a book in the SISTERS OF THE HEART SERIES.

Six women. Four decades. One long, unexpected reunion.
Book 1: Greetings from Lavender Valley
Book 2: Pathway to Lavender Valley
Book 3: Sanctuary at Lavender Valley
Book 4: Blossoms at Lavender Valley
Book 5: Comfort in Lavender Valley
Book 6: Reunion in Lavender Valley

ACKNOWLEDGMENTS

I had so much fun researching lavender recipes, along with some other foodie combinations in Lydia's story. The only downside was I made myself so hungry. If you could read this and not reach for a cookie or long for one of Lydia's special meals, you're made of strong stock.

Lydia has a bit of mystery around her and is such a free spirit. Some of her desire to roam is her own, but as you read the story, you understand more about why she never sticks around one place too long. I wanted Lydia to find the security and safety she sought and even though she didn't have a plan to stay in Lavender Valley longer than the festival, I think she's found exactly what she needs.

As Georgia arrives at the end of Lydia's story, all the sisters of the heart are home and back where Jewel hoped they would be. The festival starts soon, and all the hard work and planning will come together. I'm looking forward to sharing her story with you.

My thanks to my editor, Susan, for finding my mistakes and helping me polish *Comfort in Lavender Valley*. This gorgeous cover and all the covers in the series are the result of the talents of Elizabeth Mackey, who never disappoints. I'm fortunate to have such an incredible team helping me.

I so appreciate all of the readers who have taken the time to tell their friends about my work and provide reviews of my books. These reviews are especially important in promoting future books, so if you enjoy my novels, please consider leaving a review and sharing it on social media. I also encourage you to follow me on Amazon, Goodreads, and BookBub, where leaving a review is even easier, and you'll be the first to know about new releases and deals.

Remember to visit my website at http://www.tammylgrace.com and join my mailing list for my exclusive group of readers. I also have a fun Book Buddies Facebook Group. That's the best place to find me and get a chance to participate in my giveaways. Join my Facebook group at https://www.facebook.com/groups/AuthorTammyLGraceBookBuddies/

and keep in touch—I'd love to hear from you.

Enjoy Lavender Valley,

Tammy

MORE FROM TAMMY L. GRACE

COOPER HARRINGTON DETECTIVE NOVELS

Killer Music

Deadly Connection

Dead Wrong

Cold Killer

HOMETOWN HARBOR SERIES

Hometown Harbor: The Beginning (Prequel Novella)

Finding Home

Home Blooms

A Promise of Home

Pieces of Home

Finally Home

Forever Home

Follow Me Home

CHRISTMAS STORIES

A Season for Hope: Christmas in Silver Falls Book 1

The Magic of the Season: Christmas in Silver Falls Book 2

Christmas in Snow Valley: A Hometown Christmas Book 1

One Unforgettable Christmas: A Hometown Christmas Book 2

Christmas Wishes: Souls Sisters at Cedar Mountain Lodge

Christmas Surprises: Soul Sisters at Cedar Mountain Lodge

GLASS BEACH COTTAGE SERIES

Beach Haven

Moonlight Beach

Beach Dreams

WRITING AS CASEY WILSON

A Dog's Hope

A Dog's Chance

WISHING TREE SERIES

The Wishing Tree

Wish Again

Overdue Wishes

SISTERS OF THE HEART SERIES

Greetings from Lavender Valley

Pathway to Lavender Valley

Sanctuary at Lavender Valley

Blossoms at Lavender Valley

Comfort in Lavender Valley

Reunion in Lavender Valley

Remember to subscribe to Tammy's exclusive group of readers for your gift, only available to readers on her mailing list. **Sign up at www.tammylgrace.com. Follow this link to subscribe at https:// wp.me/P9umIy-e** and you'll receive the exclusive interview she did with all the canine characters in her Hometown Harbor Series.

Follow Tammy on Facebook by liking her page. You may also follow Tammy on book retailers or at BookBub by clicking on the follow button.

FROM THE AUTHOR

Thank you for reading COMFORT IN LAVENDER VALLEY. I love all the characters in this new SISTERS OF THE HEART SERIES and am excited for readers to get to know each of them. I started this series with a prequel book that gives readers a peek into the lives of all the women in the series. It's a great way to try it and see if the story appeals to you. Then, each subsequent book will feature each woman as the main character in her own story. Now that you've read Lydia's story, I'm anxious to share Georgia's in REUNION IN LAVENDER VALLEY. It focuses on Georgia's caring nature and creativity and includes a surprise or two.

If you enjoy women's fiction and haven't yet read the entire HOMETOWN HARBOR SERIES, you can start the series with a free prequel that is in the form of excerpts from Sam's journal. She's the main character in the first book, FINDING HOME.

If you're a new reader and enjoy mysteries, I write a series that features a lovable private detective, Coop, and his faithful golden retriever, Gus. If you like whodunits that will keep you guessing until the end, you'll enjoy the COOPER HARRINGTON DETECTIVE NOVELS.

The two books I've written as Casey Wilson, A DOG'S HOPE and A DOG'S CHANCE have received enthusiastic support from my readers, and if you're a dog lover, they are must reads.

If you enjoy holiday stories, be sure to check out my CHRISTMAS IN SILVER FALLS SERIES and HOMETOWN CHRISTMAS SERIES. They are smalltown Christmas stories of hope, friendship, and family. You won't want to miss any of the SOUL SISTERS AT CEDAR MOUNTAIN LODGE BOOKS, also featuring a foster sister theme. It's a connected Christmas series I wrote with four author friends. My contributions, CHRISTMAS WISHES, CHRISTMAS SURPRISES, and CHRISTMAS SHELTER. All heartwarming, smalltown holiday stories that I'm sure you'll enjoy. The series kicks off with a free prequel novella, CHRISTMAS SISTERS, where you'll get a chance to meet the characters during their first Christmas together.

You won't want to miss THE WISHING TREE SERIES, set in Vermont. This series centers on a famed tree in the middle of the quaint town that is thought to grant wishes to those who tie them on her branches. Readers love this series and always comment how they are full of hope, which we all need more of right now.

I'd love to send you my exclusive interview with the canine companions in my Hometown Harbor Series as a thank-you for joining my exclusive group of readers. You can sign up www.tammylgrace.com by clicking this link: https://wp.me/P9umIy-e.

ABOUT THE AUTHOR

Tammy L. Grace is the *USA Today* bestselling and award-winning author of the Cooper Harrington Detective Novels, the bestselling Hometown Harbor Series, and the Glass Beach Cottage Series, along with several sweet Christmas novellas. Tammy also writes under the pen name of Casey Wilson for Bookouture and Grand Central. You'll find Tammy online at www.tammylgrace.com where you can join her mailing list and be part of her exclusive group of readers. Connect with Tammy on Facebook at www.facebook.com/tammylgrace.books or Instagram at @authortammylgrace.

- facebook.com/tammylgrace.books
- twitter.com/TammyLGrace
- instagram.com/authortammylgrace
- bookbub.com/authors/tammy-l-grace
- goodreads.com/tammylgrace
- amazon.com/author/tammylgrace

Made in the USA
Middletown, DE
17 August 2023